Two Days At Two Dogs

A Western Novel

Bob Schaffer

iUniverse, Inc.
New York   Bloomington

Two Days At Two Dogs
A Western Novel

iUniverse books may be ordered through booksellers or by contacting:

iUniverse
1663 Liberty Drive
Bloomington, IN 47403
www.iuniverse.com
1-800-Authors (1-800-288-4677)

ISBN: 978-0-595-52108-1 (pbk)
ISBN: 978-0-595-50971-3 (cloth)
ISBN: 978-0-595-62172-9 (ebk)

Printed in the United States of America

Dedication

This is for my Mom, Fran, who always insisted that I speak and write well. Unfortunately, she left us in 2006.

Acknowledgements

I would like to thank *Ed Little* for kick-starting me on this novel and for the advice he gave on some of the technical aspects. I would also like to thank *Jack Ingebrigtsen* for spurring me on to the completion of this project.

Chapter 1

A bright and full moon shone down on the prairie, creating long, sharp shadows that were eerie and surreal. The autumn moon was its fullest, giving the wide prairie an aura of subtle loneliness. Only the chuck of a prairie dog, or the infrequent sound of a bird, broke the stillness and the sound of a horse and a mule making their way through the still night.

The sound of the hoof beats came first; then, slowly the figure of a man on horseback came over the rise. A slow, tiring; pace that came steadily onward. The rider, horse, and the mule moved with heads down, sleepy and trail weary.

The year is 1888 and Wade Dellums is the man in the saddle. Dellums, a cowboy, rancher and rifle salesman, had been riding south for the last two days. A week earlier, he had been riding west to Missoula from a successful sales trip in the Dakotas, intent on getting to his ranch in the Bitterroot Valley for some much-needed rest. His friend, Ben, had written two weeks earlier that he was having some trouble and needed Wade's help. Although the letter was somewhat cryptic about what kind of trouble Ben was having, Wade knew Ben well enough to know if Ben needed help - there was big trouble!

Wade had rested overnight, reprovisioned his supplies and changed to his favorite horse, Lightfoot. He then rode out again, only this time he was heading south to Idaho's Lemhi Valley, where Ben's ranch was located. Yesterday, Wade had come through the south-end of the Bitterroot Valley, a rich, fertile valley formed by the Sapphire and Bitterroot mountain ranges. At the end of the valley, the mountains rose and Wade crossed them over the Lost Trail Pass, working his way down from the nearly seven thousand foot pass carefully, for the back side of the mountain was steep and treacherous.

He was riding in the valley now, using the Lemhi River as a reference guide. As he rode on, Wade's mind wandered from thought-to-thought, for there little for him to do, but sit the saddle and think. His mind settles on his recent life as a Winchester salesman, and on his seemingly endless travels around the West. He feels a little like a tumbleweed in strong wind - always moving in one direction and then another - his direction determined by his employers.

At thirty years of age, Wade knew he should settle in to his ranch, maybe get married and raise a family; however, a nagging wanderlust seemed to prevail. His ranch in the Bitterroots had belonged to his parents and after their deaths, the ranch had become his. He tried ranching at first and had worked hard at it. While he enjoyed a moderate success for his initial efforts, Wade's wanderlust re-emerged, taunting him on to this nomadic existence. He had put the ranch in the capable hands of his foreman, who had worked many years for his Dad, and hit the trail selling Winchester Repeating Arms. That had been more than two years ago and here he was in the middle of practically nowhere, on a journey to help a friend in trouble. This nagging doubt about his life wasn't a new occurrence, but each time it happened, the entire train of thought unsettled him and left him depressed.

With a slight shake of his head, Wade cleared his mind. Instead, he moved his thoughts to his friend, Ben Taylor. He rolled Ben's nickname, "Two Dogs", over in his mind. Ben had gotten his nickname in his teen years in Montana. The nickname had stuck and most folks, to this day, called him "Two Dogs Taylor" No one knew why Ben was called Two Dogs - No one, except Wade Dellums, that is!

Wade knew its origins, for he had given Ben the nickname when they were both teenagers. He smiled a mischievous smile as he recalled the day, so many years ago, when he had given Ben the nickname.

They both had reached the ripe old age of fourteen and thought of themselves as men, able to conquer the world. Boys that age, Wade knew now, have more bravado than good sense. They thought of themselves as young virile men, who could do anything they set their minds to.

The morning of the nicknaming had followed a Saturday night dance at the Grange Hall. Ben and Wade had danced a lot that evening; however, Ben seemed to disappear frequently with his dancing partners. After a time, Wade decided to check on Ben's whereabouts. He slipped out of the hall and looked around the wagons and horses tied-up out front. He saw no sight of Ben. Then he heard some giggles coming from a small barn that served the Grange members for hay and general storage.

Approaching the barn quietly, Wade lifted the door latch noiselessly and peered in through the door crack. There, in the hay, lay Ben and a young girl named Margaret. They were kissing and rolling about in the hay. Wade watched, but made no sound. It was plain to see Ben was getting nowhere in his efforts with Margaret. He could see the frustration on Ben's face. He smiled, quietly closed the door and returned to the dance.

Wade was dancing with a girl named Sarah, when he spotted Ben and Margaret slipping in the side door. It wasn't long before Wade's eye caught Ben and a girl called Matilda heading for the side door. Probably making for the barn again, he thought. A few minutes later, he retraced his steps to the barn. Again, he lifted the latch, pulling the door open a crack. He couldn't believe what he saw. It was exactly the same scene as before, only the girl had changed. And, once again, Ben was frustrating over his failed efforts as a lover. Matilda, while she might consent to a peck on the cheek, wasn't tolerating Ben's more amorous advances. He heard the small crack of a slap on the face as he closed the door; stifling a laugh, he returned to the dance.

As Ben and Wade were riding home after the dance, Wade asked, "Say Ben, where did you keep disappearing to all evening long?" I looked for you a number of times and couldn't find you?"

"Hell Wade, I was out in the barn makin' love," Ben drawled, with a sheepish grin.

"How many times did you go out to the barn?"

"I guess I was out there three or four times or so."

"You go out there with the same girl every time?"

"Naw, I had a different girl every time", Ben beamed.

"I'd say you're becoming quite a lover, don't you think?"

"I'd say you're right, Wade. I am quite a lover."

"Yeh, I guess you are. You must be tired, what with the dancin' and all the foolin' around in the barn?"

"Hell, Wade, I'm not tired! You know how strong I am."

"I guess the point is - Did you do any good out there in the barn, Ben?" Wade challenged, leading Ben on even more.

"Of course I did! You know me; a big charming lover, that's me."

Wade chuckled and they rode the rest of the way home in silence.

The next morning, the boys had ridden to church with their families. After the services, the boys rode home together. Ben started to brag some about his amorous exploits of the night before.

"You know, Wade? Them girls in town 'jes can't resist me. I sure had fun last night."

"That's not the way I saw it, Chum" Wade said with a big smile beaming across the whole of his face.

What do you mean? -- the way you saw it?" Ben said concern in his voice now.

Hell, Ben, I sneaked out to the barn twice to see what you were up to."

"Damn you - You rat! Spying on a friend when he's makin' some love."

"Shit!" Wade exclaimed. "You call that makin' love? Rolling around in the hay - getting your hands and face slapped -- that's makin' love?

"Some pal you are, spying on a guy," Ben sniggered, his ego now totally deflated.

Wade retreated a little, saying, "I wasn't really spying, just seeing what you were up to."

They rode along in silence for a time, then Wade laughed, "You know, Ben, you were so frustrated at not getting anywhere with the girls -- it was kind'a funny. Shit, you reminded me of two dogs tryin' to screw in a lighting storm. Yup, that's what you reminded me of --two dogs screwin'! I'm goin' to call you that from now on -- 'Ol Two Dogs Taylor -- that's who you are."

Damn you, Wade! Some friend," Ben snapped back, "If you call me that, then everyone will know about last night."

"Hell, I won't tell them, Two Dogs, and I know you won't. I'd say that'll be our little secret."

Wade laughed and they rode until they came to Ben's parent's place. As Wade rode off toward his Dad's ranch, he called back to Ben, "See you tomorrow, Two Dogs!"

Dellum's mind jerked back to the present. A big smile covered his square face, as he thought – That's how legends are made – with a good nickname. He laughed out loud. The sound of his laughter echoed in the still night air.

He rode for a great while, aware of every night sound. Traveling the West had taught Wade to be alert and watchful for any danger. Before long, his eyes spotted what appeared to be a campfire up the trail and off to the right at some distance. When he'd ridden closer, he could see it was a campfire and, it appeared, there were several cowboys in the camp.

He turned his horse off the trail and approached the camp. At a proper distance, Wade stopped his horse and hailed the camp, "Hello, the camp!"

"Hello, who's out there?" came the reply.

"Wade Dellums from Montana, ridin' south. Been in the saddle a long way. Sure could use some coffee, if you got any"

"C'mon in rider – we got plenty"

Wade inched his horse toward the camp edge. He secured both the horse and mule to some brush and walked into the cowboy's camp.

"Sure appreciate you invitin' me in. Been in that saddle for three long days now", Wade mentioned as he moved forward to warm his hands by the fire.

"Where you headin' for?" one of the men asked.

"I'm headin' for White Willow, any idea how much farther it is?"

"You got several more hours in that saddle 'afore ya' get there."

The tall cowboy looked Wade over. Saying, "Name's Dellums, huh? Don't think I ever heard of ya' before. Ya' got business in White Willow or somethin'?"

"I have some business there. I sell Winchester rifles."

"Winchesters, huh? That's a good rifle. Got me one myself. Wouldn't part with it."

Wade grinned, "Most folks like the arm. I sell a lot of them."

"Well, relax, Dellums. Here have some beans. We like to think of them as "Mexican Strawberries" They're still hot," and he plopped a good-sized portion onto a tin plate.

"Me, Ed and Barney here work for the Circle T Ranch. The Circle T is near White Willow. We're on our way back there – Been up to Salmon for a couple of days, raisin' some hell. We're due in tomorrow."

"Feels good to be outa' the saddle," Wade admitted, "My butts saddle-weary."

'Well, rest yourself and eat those beans."

Dellums leaned back with his plate and ate leisurely, as the cowboys began to talk among themselves.

"We get back, I reckon "Ol Charlie will have us on that rancher again," the tall cowboy said to the other two.

The second cowboy shook his head and drawled, "Damn, but ah don't think anything'll move that man. He's dead set on staying on the land, no matter what Charlie offers."

"Cheer up, Ed" the third man offered, "Maybe Ol Charlie's had some luck with 'em while we were gone."

Wade sat quietly, eating his beans, but listening and watching intently. The tall man, remembering Wade's presence looked over and explained, "Our boss, Charlie Tate, he runs the Circle T spread, has eye on a small ranch 'jes south of the Circle T, but the rancher won't sell to him. His refusals are driving Tate wild! Charlie Tate's not the sort to take "no" for answer. One of these days, there'll be hell to pay – you can count on that!"

The second cowboy added, "Ain't no tellin' what Tate will do if he doesn't get his way! Christ, but he's a mean 'ol fart. He like to get us killed one of these days, you know that?"

After a bit, Dellums unfolded his long legs and stood up. He thanked the cowboys for the coffee and beans, adding, "It was good talking to folks again. Ah been talkin' to that horse and mule for too long. Ah'd best be heading out for White Willow. Like to get there just after sunup. Ya' know the name of the hard goods dealer in White Willow?"

"His name's Sam, Sam Miller," the tall man responded, "Ya' go see Sam at Miller's Mercantile. Ya' can't miss it. It's the only one in town – down at the center of the main street."

"Thanks," Wade said, as he untied his animals, "If I see you boys in town, I'll buy you a drink or two. It'll be on me." He mounted Lightfoot and turned out of the camp and headed south again.

Riding into the still night again, Dellums turned his thoughts to the conversations he'd heard in the cowboy's camp. A thought kept nagging at him. *Could the small rancher be his friend, Ben Taylor?* The cowboys never mentioned the rancher by name. Wade pondered and speculated about the rancher's name; however, he wasn't able to come to a conclusion, because he knew too little of the facts. He decided he'd hang around White Willow for a day or two, sell some rifles, and pick up what local gossip he could. Maybe he could learn what sort of trouble Two Dogs was having. He rode on through the moonlit night, pondering the things he had heard.

The sun was just breaking the eastern horizon as he crested the final ridge that lay a few miles above White Willow. Wade looked down a long, rolling valley and saw the town, which lay off-center to the west. It lay a long a small, dry river. He had heard White Willow's primary business was cattle and that it was a growing town, with some mining activity springing up northwest of town

The town, now quiet in the early hours, appeared to have a dozen or more buildings along the main street. It wasn't unlike most of the towns Wade had traveled to in his journeys around the West. He spurred Lightfoot on for the last stretch into White Willow.

Chapter 2

The sun was rising, casting long shadows from the buildings on Wade's right, as he guided Lightfoot up White Willow's main street. Early morning activity was beginning – a sleepy town stirring itself awake after a long autumn night.

He rode slowly, causing little notice from the few folks on the street at this time of the morning. White Willow had a bank, a telegraph office, a land office, two saloons, a number of shops of various kinds, a sheriff's office, a livery stable and two small hotels. In the center of town was Miller's Mercantile, just as the cowboy had directed.

Wade was pleased to see the livery stable located only a few doors away from one of the hotels. After so many days in the saddle, the thought of having to haul his heavy pack saddle panniers and manties any distance wearied him. The two manties were very heavy, for they carried his sample Winchesters. He decided to register at the hotel first, unload the horse and mule, and then he would take them both down to the livery stable. He turned the animals around and headed for Chalmer's Hotel & Saloon.

He approached the hotel registration desk and was greeted by a tall, thin woman who seemed self-assured and totally in charge of the hotel's operations. He asked for a room for a few days. She assured him there were plenty of rooms available, this being the slow time of the week.

Dellums smiled a pleasant smile, a smile he reserved for the ladies, and said, "This the first time I've been to White Willow. It sure looks like a nice town."

"We like it," she quipped, without a sarcastic note in her voice. "Ned and me have been here since Sixty-Four, when the town was started. We put this place together, board by board. My name's Betty, Betty Chalmers."

"I'm Wade Dellums, from up Missoula way. I've a ranch in the Bitterroots."

"A rancher, eh? What brings you to White Willow, Mr. Dellums?"

"Well, I am a rancher, but a kind'a footloose one, 'cause I travel around selling rifles and ammunition. That's why I'm here in White Willow – to sell some rifles."

"I guess this is as good a place as any to sell some rifles," she responded, adding, "You'll be calling on Sam Miller across the way at the Mercantile then?"

"Yes Mam, are there many ranchers around here?"

"Yes, Mr. Dellums, we've a lot of ranches in the area, plus there are some small mining operations to the south. Business has gotten much better in the last few years."

"Well, that's good news, Mam. A salesman always worries about there won't be enough customers around town to buy his wares."

"What kind of rifle do you sell?" she asked.

"I sell Winchesters, Mrs. Chalmers. Folks seem to like them, so's my work isn't too hard."

"Please call me Betty," she smiled for the first time." "Ned will be happy. He has an old Sharps rifle. He's been talking about a new Winchester lately. He'll probably be one of the first customers to buy one, Mr. Dellums."

"Please call me Wade, Betty," Wade grinned, "He's probably wanting our model '86. It has been right popular with folks. Well, I guess I'd better get to unloadin' that 'ol mule."

"I'd better give you your room key. I've put you in the upper front room. It has a good view of the street. It's our best room. Enjoy your stay in White Willow, Wade."

It took two trips to his room, lugging the panniers and manties up the creaky stairs. When everything was up in his room, Wade led the animals to the livery stables.

The sign over the door said, "Livery Stables, Amos Hart, Prop." Wade walked in the doorway and saw an older man, currying a chestnut mare.

"Howdy," Wade said, still leading the animals.

"Howdy Stranger," the man said, putting up his curry comb and walked toward Wade.

"I'd like to put my animals up for a couple of days, if you got room for them?"

"Sure do – fact, I have plenty of room for 'em," he said, and then he eyed the horse and mule, "Been on the trail long?"

"Yah, three or four days. Came down from the Bitterroots. Name's Dellums, Wade Dellums."

"Pleased to meet ya' Dellums. My name's
Amos Hart, like the signs says. Most folks hereabouts 'jes call me Amos."

"Well, call me Wade. I'm in White Willow on some business. Should be here two, three days at the most."

"What kind'a business ya' got in White Willow? You some kind'a salesman or sumthin'?"

"Yup, you got me there, Amos. I'm a salesman. What did they call 'em after the War" – a carpetbagger? I sell Winchester rifles."

"Winchester, huh? That's a mighty fine arm. Been wantin' one of those myself, not that I need it. I never seem to get out of here anymore. Still'n all, it would be nice to have in case of trouble. Not that there's much of that anymore. Still'in all, be nice to have a Winchester, just in case.. S'pose you'll be callin' on Sam Miller?"

"Yup," Wade replied, "What kinda' man is Sam? This is the first time I've come to White Willow."

"You'll like Sam, he's a darn right nice fella'. He's been here for a long time – knows most all the folks hereabouts.

Runs a good store. You can find most anything you're needin' in there."

"Amos," Wade said, turning to his animals. "This here's Lightfoot, she's a well mannered horse, and that there is Marybelle. She won't give you any problems. As mules go, Marybelle's a sweetheart!"

"They won't have any problems with me. Critters and me get on well. Fact, sometimes I like critters better'n people. Treat critters right and they treat you right. Not like some people I met in my day."

"You're right about that, Amos," Wade said as he began loosen Lightfoot's latigo.

"Here now," Amos interrupted, "Let me get that. Got nuthin' to do anyways. Your saddle and tack'll be right here," he said, pointing to a rack just outside the stall where Lightfoot would be.

"Have yourself a nice stay in White Willow," Amos Hart offered, then added with a smile, "Go sell 'Ol Sam a lot of Winchesters."

Wade thanked him and headed back to the hotel. As he walked along the side street to the corner, Wade noticed the hotel saloon. The hotel faced the main street and the saloon faced the side street, its space fitted neatly into the back of the hotel structure. It must have been built after the hotel was constructed, Wade decided as he viewed the structure.

Dellums entered and walked toward the bar. He placed some coins in front of him and ordered a whisky. The bartender has his back to the bar and was busy polishing the large plate glass mirror that was part of the backbar. He turned and eyed Wade, then walked down the bar where he poured Wade a whiskey.

The bartender was tall, middle-aged and his white apron failed to hide the pot belly that hung about his waist.

"You must be new in town, Stranger?" the bartender said matter-of-factly.

"Yup, I am, I just checked in to the hotel a little while ago," Wade said, raising the glass to his lips.

"Ah, you be the Winchester man that came in this mornin'. My wife said she talked with you some. My name's Ned, Ned Chalmers. We own the hotel and saloon." He offered his hand across the bar.

"Glad to know you. Name's Wade, Wade Dellums," Wade said, shaking Ned's hand firmly, and yes, I do sell Winchester Repeating Arms. Your wife said you have been wanting one of the new models." Wade gestured to his glass, "Guess you best fill this up again, Ned."

Ned refilled the glass, placing the bottle on the bar. "I've had a Sharps for some time now. Kind'a thought it'd be nice to have a repeating rifle. Mentioned that fact to Betty a couple of times now – you gotta' kinda' sell her on these things' She watches our purse strings pretty close. Spendin' forty dollars for a rifle isn't easy for her. Can't complain though, wouldn't have a damn thing if it hadn't been for her. That woman's darn good with a dollar."

"My mother was like that too, she kept my 'ol man on the straight and narrow. He liked to gamble – that was his failin' – she kept a tight rein on the money. I'd guess he never would'a had the ranch if it wasn't for her."

"She sounds like my Betty. We wouldn't have had the hotel or this place if it weren't for her. We did it piece by piece, dollar by dollar. And we don't owe no one for it. Kinda' makes a man proud, don't it?"

"It sure would me, I know," Wade said, tipping up his second shot of whisky. As he did so, the weariness of the long hours on the trail came over him. He knew it was time for some sleep.

"Well, Ned, I gotta' get some sleep – all that saddle time comin' south from Missoula has caught up with me. I'll see you later on."

Wade went around the corner to the hotel entrance. As he walked up the stairs, he nodded to Betty Chalmers, who was at the front desk working on the books. Once in his room, Wade looked out his front window for a moment, then he headed for the bed. Sleep couldn't wait any longer!

Chapter 3

It was nearly one o'clock, the sun high, when
Wade awoke with a start. At first, he thought he'd slept
the day around, but after checking the sun, he decided he'd
only slept for about four hours.

He lay staring at the ceiling for a long while, his thoughts
mulling over Two Dog's trouble and whether or not it had
anything to with the Charlie Tate he had heard the cowboys
talking about last night. He kicked these thoughts around
in his mind for a time, then decided he had to nose around
town some more and see what he could find out about
Charlie Tate. He realized the best place to start looking for
information was at Miller's Mercantile.

Miller's was located diagonally across the street from the
hotel. From his window, Wade could see the activity across
the street. Miller's was a busy store. The building was quite
large, with a loading dock on the side street for feed and
ranch supplies. He could see items like barbed wire, tools,

and sacks of flour or grain being loaded into customer's wagons.

He turned from the window, deciding it was time to get his rifle sales materials ready. He placed the two canvass manties on the bed and untied the lines that held the parcels together. As the canvass came loose, he unrolled the oilskin covering that protected the rifles from moisture. When he was finished, he had six Winchesters of various calibers, plus a number of cartridge boxes for the different calibers, including some cartridges loaded with the new smokeless powder.

After working the action of each of the rifles, he carefully wiped them down, removing any excess oil. Wade took one of the panniers, which were actually large leather and canvass satchel-type bags designed for loading on the tree of the mule rigging. From the pannier he fished out a large piece of dark blue flannel material. He spread the material flat on the bed. He put the first rifle on the material and rolled it once. On successive rolls, he had all the rifles rolled in the flannel. He'd show the rifles to Sam Miller in the order they unrolled from the flannel. He put the flannel parcel in the pannier. He also threw in the cartridges, fitting them along the inside. Last, he put a couple of Winchester catalogs and an order book in the bag.

He washed with cool water in the hand basin, wishing it were a hot, leisurely bath. He changed out of his trail clothes and dressed in the clothes he customarily wore in town – black pants, a white shirt of the western style, a dark kerchief tie and a leather vest with silver conchos. He out on his hat and checked his image in the mirror. Because he was a tall man, Wade had to bend low to see the top of his head and hat. Satisfied with what he saw, Wade hoisted the heavy satchel and headed for Miller's Mercantile.

A small bell tinkled as Wade opened the door to Miller's, then it tinkled again as he stepped in and closed the door. Miller's was like all general-type stores, filled with every necessity and some of the luxuries of western life. The store had a smell that was totally unique to a general store. An eager curiosity overwhelmed as he glanced around the store; a feeling he knew came from his days as a child, always dazzled by the wonders and smells of a general store. The feeling was still there after all these years! Interesting, Wade thought.

There were several customers in the store. Wade stood to the side for a time, then walked slowly about the store, looking at the broad variety of the merchandise in stock. A man and a woman worked behind the well-worn wooden counter. They both wore denim aprons and seemed to know where every item in the building was located. When Sam Miller was without a customer, he turned to Wade, who was standing near the counter now. Wade identified and introduced himself, telling Miller he was here to show him the new Model 1886 Winchester Repeating Rifles.

"Well. It's about time. I've been waitin' for someone to come callin'. I'm Sam Miller and that lady over there is my wife, Helen," he said. As he turned and called to her;"Helen, tell Arthur to come in from the dock and give a hand. I'm goin' to spend some time with the Winchester man." Gesturing to the far end of the long counter, Miller said," How about we go down to the end – no one will bother us much down there."

Wade half-carried and half-slid his heavy satchel down to the end of the counter, saying as he went along,"Ya' know, Mr. Miller, this is the first time I've ever been to White Willow."

'Wade, you can call me Sam, everybody else does. That mister stuff sounds silly around here.'

'Sam it is then. I really like your store. You seem to have anything a body'd need in here," Wade said, as he turned and glanced around the building."

"Glad you like it. It has taken us years to get this much merchandise variety in inventory. Most folks can find what they are looking for in here.

Wade unrolled the flannel containing the new rifles. He unrolled the flannel just enough to expose the first rifle. "Here's the new Winchester Model '86 carbine, 45-60-caliber," he spoke knowingly, holding it up, working the lever action. He handed it to Sam.

Sam hefted it and worked the lever action several times, then sighted down the barrel as though aiming at a target. "This arm sure feels good in the hand – its got good balance, ought to fire well from the saddle."

'Not only does feel good in the hands, this new carbine fires accurately – fast and accurate repeating fire. Beyond all doubt, it's the best repeating arm on the market today. What we should do is take it out somewhere and fire it, so you can see and judge for yourself," Wade said, sounding very much the salesman. The thought always amused Wade, for he didn't feel like a salesman. Anyway selling Winchesters was easy – they sold themselves.

"Well, we can do that, ya' know! There's a wash just outside of town that folks use for rifle and revolver practice. We'll go out there and give this Winchester a real tryout," Miller beamed, but his attention was drawn to the other end of the counter, where his son Arthur, was having some trouble with a customer. Turning away from Wade, Sam Miller walked slowly over the Arthur and two men were arguing.

"What seems to be the problem here, Charlie?" Miller asked the older, heavier man.

"Christ a'mighty Sam, I ordered those ready-made saddles weeks ago and they are not here yet," the heavy man growled, gesturing with his hands, "Where the hell are they comin' from? - China?," he added.

"Charlie, you know those saddles were ordered out of Denver, and – by all rights, they should have been here by now. I'm not exactly sure what happened to them."

"Damn, I've a ranch to run and I need those damned saddles. Shit, I could'a rode to Denver myself in all this time."

"Look Charlie, I'll telegraph the firm in Denver today and we'll see what's happened to the order. Then, we'll know for sure," Miller advised him in an appeasing tone of voice.

The man, Charlie, simmered down some and said, "Well, if you could do that Sam, I'd be mighty pleased. I need those saddles."

"Then, that's what we will do, Charlie," Sam said, turning to his son, "Arthur, pull Mr. Tate's order from the file and I'll telegraph Denver myself."

"Thank you, Sam," Charlie Tate said, and stormed out of the store, the second man scurrying along to keep up with him.

Wade watched the encounter over the saddles quietly from the side. *So that's Charlie Tate?* He thought. *He's not very likeable, that's f'sure.* His thoughts were interrupted when Sam Miller returned to Wade's end of the counter.

"Let's get goin' Wade, before we have any more interruptions. I've a buckboard out at the side," he said, as he started for the side door. Wade picked up his satchel and followed Sam out.

Sam Miller was silent as they rode out of town. He seemed to be mulling over the events of the heated conversation with Charlie Tate. As they neared the wash, Sam said in exasperation, "Damn, that man Tate! He riles me every time I have to do business with him. He argued with me when he placed the order – he argued with me about the shipping time then – and, he's been in every week since to raise hell about the saddles. Naturally, somethin's got to go wrong on the Denver end, and that man leaves me no peace of mind!"

'What kinda' man is he, Sam - that he feels he has to shout and order folks around so?" Wade asked, his face set hard with an inquiring look.

"Tate's probably the most disliked man around town, mainly because of his rough manners and terrible temper. Most folks give him a wide berth, for he's not the easiest man to deal with. He's got a good-sized ranch southwest of here. It's called the Circle T. Some say he's acquiring more and more land to add to the ranch. Most of the "acquiring" is illegal. He forces small ranchers off their land by hazing and harassing them. If that doesn't work he threatens and scares them off. He's done that a number of times that I know of."

"How does he get away with it?" Wade asked, "Doesn't the sheriff know about this?"

Sheriff Todd knows somethin's wrong, but it has been hard to prove. Tate always has the legal papers for the transfer of the deeds. The folks he's forced out are usually gone by the time Tate transfers the deed, so the papers go through legally, and Tate's the new owner. Zack, that's Sheriff Zack Todd, is bamboozled, because he hasn't been able to catch Tate at it."

Wade took down the Winchesters from the back of the buckboard, and handed the 45-60 to Sam. "This Charlie

Tate sure sounds like a scoundrel," Wade commented as he handed Sam some rifle cartridges.

"The gossip around town is that he's been tryin' to run off a young family located just over the mountain there," Sam said, pointing at the western mountain line, indicating a northwesterly direction with his finger.

"They're damned nice people, run a good ranch. The ranch is small, but it has an excellent water source – that's probably what 'Ol Tate has his eyes on - the water. Rancher's name is Ben Taylor. He's well-liked by folks around here. Tate's been after him for some time now, but Taylor just says no. That gets Tate riled as hell. I heard Tate's boys been harassing Taylor, ya' know – cuttin' fences, scattering the herd and things like that.

"Well Sam, let's do some shooting," Wade said, changing the subject. He walked down range and placed several empty cartridge boxes along the bank. He found a number of empty bottles and placed them along the bank too.

"Sam, you'll notice how easily the Model '86 sights. Draw a bead on one of the bottles and squeeze 'er off."

Sam cocked the Winchester, leveled, sighted in, and squeezed off a round. His first shot hit the bottle dead-on.

"This carbine sure fires where you aim it. And, like I said before she feels well in hand – it has got damned good balance to it."

'When you cock it again, notice the smooth action. Now fire a couple of rounds and notice how smoothly that action allows you to come down on the same aiming point."

Miller worked the lever action slowly, checking the smooth action. He squeezed off a round, then quickly re-cocked and fired again. In a matter of seconds, he had fired four rounds. He hit each of his targets – again, dead-on.

Wade reached into his vest and pulled out several cartridges. "Sam, I have something amazing to show you! You recall the smoke you created when you fired your four rounds? The French have come up with the formula for smokeless gun powder. Try firing these rounds," and Wade handed Sam the cartridges he had in his vest.

Sam loaded the new rounds and cocked the piece, firing off several rounds. No smoke came from the barrel. Sam was amazed. "That is amazing, Wade. You say the French came up with this new gun powder?"

"Yep, that was the last of the new smokeless cartridges that I've got; however, all our cartridges will be smokeless from now on. Winchester has assured me of that."

Sam was pleased with his shooting and impressed with the new smokeless gun powder. "You know, Wade? I've never fired a smoother arm before. Should sell well and the smokeless gun powder will certainly help. You have sold me, Wade. I'd best be getting back to the store. Helen gets anxious if I'm gone too long."

On the ride back, they discussed the price of the Winchesters, the new cartridges and the delivery time from San Francisco. Sam also wanted to know if the Montgomery & Ward Company was selling the Model '86 in their catalog. Sam claimed they undersold the regular dealers by a good deal.

"As far as I have been told, Montgomery & Ward are not selling the Model '86." By that time, they were at the outskirts of town and Sam had settled on a large order of Winchesters.

Business done – Sam looked out to the approaching town, "White Willow's a nice town, Lotsa' good folks here, Wade. Don't have much riff-raff. Mostly it's Charlie Tate's boys that cause any problems. They try to rattle-up the town on the weekends, but the sheriff keeps them in line. I guess most towns are that way. We're no Dodge City, or Abilene, that's f'sure."

"You sound like you ought to be the Mayor of White Willow," Wade chuckled, chiding Sam a bit.

"Been thinking about that myself, Wade," Sam said with a wink and a laugh! He reined-in to the loading dock at the side of the store. "C'mon, let's fill out the order. I've got some work to do."

Chapter 4

W ade walked slowly on the board sidewalk along the block of buildings north of his hotel., the hollowness below the boards creating an echo that gave dimension to the movement of his boots.

It was dark. The sun had disappeared in the western sky more than an hour ago. The only lights that filtered out onto the street were the lights from the hotels and saloons. A few stores showed a light, but they would soon be extinguished as the owners locked up for the night.

He'd fallen asleep in his room after his sales call on Sam Miller. He had awakened in the failing afternoon light, fearing he'd slept the night away. It was a relief when he realized he'd only slept a couple of hours. *Damn!* he thought, *that's twice today I've awakened like that. Gonna' have to catch up my sleep one of these days.*

Nearing the corner of the block, he spotted his destination. A saloon called the "Palace", or more correctly, "Murphy's Palace Saloon" Although well-lit by lamps, the saloon was a typical cow town saloon, dusty and well-worn – peopled mostly by cowhands.

The folks in the bar eyed him carefully as he walked to the far end of the bar. Dellums was used to this, for a traveling man is always the stranger – the new man in town, no matter what town he traveled to. He leaned against the bar and ordered a whisky.

The bartender was a large, well-built man, with dark eyes, and a demeanor that made one feel he could eat nails. He looked Wade over as he poured the whiskey.

"You must be new in town, Stranger?" he said as he pushed the whiskey glass to Wade. "I can't say as I've seen you in here before."

"You're right. I just got to town today. I've some business with Sam Miller. I sell Winchester rifles."

"Yeah, Yeah! I heard there was a Winchester man in town, that's you, huh?"

"Yup, that's me. Name's Dellums, Wade Dellums", he said, offering his hand, "You the proprietor?"

The big man leaned over the bar pushing forward a big, meaty hand that engulfed Wade's when he shook it. "My names Mike, Mike Murphy and the saloon is mine, such as it is."

"It's a nice place," Wade lied, "Not unlike a lot of saloons here in the West. You know, a place to rest and blow the trail dust out of your throat."

"Well, we gotta' a rough crowd here. Damn cowboys always lookin' for a fight. You know what I mean, they get a little liquored-up and they think they can lick the whole damn town. Saturday nights can be hard on a man's nerves. Sheriff's around a lot on Saturdays, with a deputy. They lock most of them and let them sleep it off."

"Seems quiet tonight," Wade said, looking around the long room – noticing a few customers, all engaged in quiet conversations.

"It'll be noisier later tonight. The more drinks they get under their belts, the nosier they get – never fails," Murphy said with a smile, then he asked, "How long you been selling for the Winchester outfit?"

"I don't actually work for the Winchester Repeating Arms Company in New Haven, Connecticut. I work for their distributor out of San Francisco – a firm called, Howard

& Kahler. They hired me about two years ago to sell the Winchester Model '86 repeating arms and ammunition. Ya' know, to introduce the new models to the West. Most folks think I work directly for Winchester but I don't really."

"I guess that's interesting work. Getting' around the West and talkin' with a lot of folks."

"Well, I like the movin' around part and the meetin' of new people – but damn, there's a lot of long, lonely trails between towns. You'd think you would get used to it, but mostly you don't. There's something very impersonal about a hotel room in a strange new town. Guess you gotta' take the good with the bad."

"Yeh, I guess you do. Ya' know, I never looked at it like that. I get so tied up here in this saloon. I hanker to get some trial dust in my mouth – if you get my drift. Oh, I do alright here – it just that I tend to feel trapped behind this bar. A shot of the open spaces could be a great relief. That is the way it is, isn't it? There's good and bad in everything we do. Life's never easy, is it?"

"I'd guess not," Wade nodded solemnly, " Someday soon I'd better settle in and quit being a wanderer."

Murphy poured another whiskey and left to serve some cowboys who had just come in. Wade sipped his whiskey and thought about his day. He learned a little about "Two Dog's" problem – Charlie Tate and his boys were serious about running him off his land. He wondered what they were going to do next."

Wade was standing, face forward to the bar, with his back to the rest of the room and he was very much engrossed in his thoughts about "Two Dog's." He didn't notice the group of cowhands that came in and were sitting down to the poker table at his right rear.

He kept thinking about the conversations he'd over heard last night in the cowboy camp. From what he could figure out from the conversations, it was really a simple matter – Charlie Tate wanted "Two Dog's" ranch no matter what. The cowboys themselves, although a rough and ragged bunch, were apprehensive about Tate's future actions to get the ranch. There was no question about the urgency of Tate's desires to get he ranch.

He'd seen Tate in action at Sam Miller's, and remembered Miller's remarks about Charlie Tate. They showed Tate as unliked by most folks and, more than likely, feared by the same folks because of his rough, direct manner and his uneven handiness which he handled both people and business. He definitely wasn't a man to trust.

"Ya' ready for another?" Wade looked up from his thoughts to see Murphy standing there, the whisky bottle poised and ready to pour.

'You bet, Mike. The darned glass doesn't do much good sittin' there empty, does it?"

"I figured you'd be ready. Sorry to run off like that, but you gott'a take care of business, ya' know," Mike reported with a smile, pouring a full measure to the glass. He did it with much flourish, leaving the amber-colored whiskey shimmering on the edge of the thick glass.

"Hey, Winchester Man," a voice from the rear of the room called out. "Hey, Winchester Man," the voice called again, after Wade didn't respond to the first call. The second time acknowledged, turning his head around to see who was calling him. It was the cowhands from last night. There were four of them tonight and they were seated around a poker table.

"How're you fella's doin'? Wade drawled with a wave of his hand, I see you made it on in alright.'"

'You bet we made it in alright – but; Boy, our throats are sure dry!" The tall hand said. He was the one who did most of the talking last night, Wade recalled.

Dellums smiles, remembering his promise to buy the boys some drinks. "Mike, how about giving the boys a bottle? I met them on the trail last, I owe them some hospitality."

Mike moved closer to the bar and spoke in an undertone, "Wade, I'd be careful with those boys – they can be a handful. Those are Charlie Tate's boys and if you aren't careful. They can be all sorts of trouble to ya'"

Wade looked Mike straight in the eye, "I hear what you're saying, but let me handle this, Mike. Shit, I owe them the drinks. Best, you let me take the bottle over there."

"Just you remember, Wade – I warned you. You be mighty careful with those boys."

Wade swooped up the bottle turned and took it over to the grinning cowhands sitting around the poker table. "I guess you do look a little thirsty," Wade said as he put the bottle on the table

----

The sun is setting in the western sky. Long shadows covered "Two Dog's" ranch house as it receded behind the mountains, leaving the pastures below dark.

Ben Taylor stands at the corral, talking with his hired hand, Seth Johnson. "Seth, I don't feel easy! I know we haven't heard the last from Charlie Tate. And I trust him about as far as I can throw that sorrel mare of yours. I know he's upta' somethin' but, I don't know what, that's what's bothers' me."

"I have the same kinda' feeling, Ben, like it's too quiet," Seth admitted. He turned to look out over the pasture; "I think it was a good idea to bring the cows into the close-in pasture. Leastways, now we can an eye on them. Don't want Tate's boys runnin' 'em off again. Seems like it took forever roundin' them critters up after the last time they scattered them."

"Two Dogs" nodded in agreement, saying, "There's not much grass left in that pasture now. I guess we'll have to start throwing them some hay 'til we get this thing settled with Tate. Another thing Seth, start keeping your shotgun in the barn – might come in handy should Tate and his boys show up looking for trouble."

They started for the house. Ben had his arm around Seth's shoulder as he said, "By the way, Seth, we should be getting' some help soon. I wrote my old partner and friend, Wade, about three weeks ago. He's up Missoula-way, ya' know. He sells rifles, Winchesters, I think."

"Three weeks ago, huh? He should be here by now, if he got the letter."

'Well, I don't know - he travels a lot and we might have missed him with the letter. One thing I know is, if he got the letter – he'd light out like a scared jack rabbit to get here. I know that f'sure, 'cause it's exactly what I do if he needed help. Seth, he'll be here, you can count on it."

From the front porch, they watched the cows grazing in the fading light for moment, and then they turned and went into the house.

Chapter 5

Wade stood before the mirror, the morning sun awash in his room. He poured fresh water in the basin, while he checked his face in the oval mirror. *Damn,* he thought, *these nights in the bar will make an old man out of me.* He picked up the bar of soap and began to wash his face and neck.

The cool water felt good on his face. It served not only to wake up his body – but also to bring his mind fully awake and alert. As he washed his upper arms and torso, he thought of the night before and the events in Murphy's Saloon.

He found he genuinely liked Mike Murphy. It was something that surprised Wade more than he found imagine. Wade's experience with saloon owners was such that he had never found one he could like, much less trust. Not so with Murphy. He seemed honest and forthright, just a man running a saloon in a rough trade. He appreciated Mike's warnings about the Tate cowhands. Mike had been right, they definitely weren't to be fooled with. They were as treacherous and ruthless a bunch as he'd ever seen. They were the type that'd dry gulch a man for his saddle and tack, and do it for no other reason than the fun of it.

Wade recalled the moment he had taken the bottle over to the cowboy's table, and had said, "I guess you boys do look a little dry," as he set the bottle down on the table.

'Wal, it's about time, Winchester Man, I thought maybe you weren't going to keep your promise," the tall cowboy drawled with a grin. As he grinned, he pulled the cork from the bottle and poured himself a shot of whiskey. "Why don't you join us?" he added, motioning for Wade to sit in an empty chair.

"A man always keeps his word, and I'm a man who keeps his word," Wade stated, pulling out the chair. When he was seated, he looked at the other cowboys.

"Let's see, you don't know the boys, do you? This fella' here – is Joey Williams, you never met him – the other two you met last night. This here's Ed Baylor, and that's Mike Burney, and – of course me, I'm Bill Colter. You wanna' play some poker?

Wade nodded an acknowledgement each time Colter identified a name with a face. After, he said, "Glad to know you boys - and, yes, I could stand a little poker. At least until the money runs out."

Wade and Colter watched in silence as the other three men, each in turn gave themselves generous shots of whiskey. It was easy to see from the great smiles on their faces, that there was nothing like a free bottle of whiskey.

The first man, Joey Williams, quickly downed the shot and poured himself another, before passing the bottle to Ed Baylor. As Wade eyed Joey, he felt a gut instinct about the man. Don't trust him, his mind and gut warned. He knew from past experiences, that his first impressions – he liked to call them – gut instincts – were usually right. He's keep a close eye on Joey Williams.

"What kind'a poker we playin' here," Wade asked, fishing some coins from his vest pocket and throwing them down on the green felt of the poker table.

"We're playin' nickel and dime five card stud. It's too close to payday to play for anythin' more," Mike Burney said, as he began to shuffle he poker deck. By the time he'd finished describing the game, the cards were shuffled and cut. He began to deal. Wade could tell from the way Burney handled the cards, he had sat in on a lot of card games in his time – in fact, a great many. He manipulated the cards like a professional gambler. Wade also knew cowboys, in general, spent much of their idle time in bunkhouses across the West playing cards – as a result they became adept at card handling.

The game began with Ed Baylor betting a nickel on his jack-o-spades, which was high. Each of the players threw a nickel in the pot. Burney dealt the next card down. He was still high, so he bet again, this time raising the ante to a dime. Wade checked to the next bettor. After all the players had put in their dimes, Wade too, tossed in his dime.

"Say Bill," Wade said casually, as the cards were being dealt again, I think I saw your boss in town today, with another cowboy – 'bout as tall as you. They were in Sam Miller's place raisin' all kinds of holy hell about some ready-saddles."

"Yeh, 'Ol Charlie and Matt were in town today. Matt Weber is our foreman. A real mean and tough hombre if there ever was one. Most folks call him, Slick" – I s'pose that's why he and Charlie get along so well – they're both mean and slick!"

"Tate was a-hoppin' and hollerin' about those saddles he ordered. I thought for a moment he might punch Sam Miller, he was so mad. Miller told me later Charlie was hard to handle – said he always wanted everything he ordered right now and it wasn't always possible to get fast delivery on many of the things Tate ordered. He said he and Charlie were almost always arguing about some order or another."

Colter's fifth card was an up-card and a ten-o-diamonds. It made a pair with his first up-card, a ten-o-hearts. With a pair of tens showing, Colter was high, so he bet a dime, only to have Joey bump it another dime. The bet was twenty cents to Wade, so he threw in a quarter, retrieving a nickel from the pot.

"Charlie Tate's none to easy on folks. He means to have his way, come hell or high water. Lately, he's become a particular pain in the ass. Barking orders all the time, he just seems to have no patience with anyone. He's probably all worked up over the Taylor ranch deal. He can't buy the place and he can't run 'im off either. He's madder than a wet hen, Christ; we don't know what he's goin' to do nest!"

"Wal, ah'll tell ya' somethin'," Mike Burney interrupted, "Lately, I think the man's gone loco. Like I said last night, one of these days he'd like to get us all killed!"

Joey Williams bet and called. Colter showed three tens. Joey cursed and turned over three sevens. Colter had the winning hand. When he began to draw in his winning pot, Joey, now full of whiskey, accused Colter of cheating. Colter took a long slow look at Williams, after an uneasy silence said, "You'd better watch your mouth, Joey, or I'll have to remove a few of those shit-eatin' teeth of yours!"

"Christ, Colter! What the hell are the odds of you beatin' three-of-a-kind with three-of-a-kind in a five card game?" Williams spit out at Colter.

"Shut up, Joey! You don't know your ass from a hole in the ground. "Jes' shut up and play!"

Wade was silent throughout this near-violent exchange
between Colter and Joey. They played cards for a couple of hours more, with Joey sulking and making insinuations all the while. By ten o'clock the bottle was empty and another was brought. Joey, his eyelids half-closed from the whiskey, called with two jacks showing. Colter turned over his cards and showed a pair of aces. He reached from the pot.

"Damn you, Colter, you're cheatin'," snarled
Williams, rising from the chair with an angry, desperate look on his face; his hand starting for his holster.

Colter, seeing the action, balled his left hand into a fist, swinging it with amazing accuracy into Joey's mouth, mashing Joey's teeth, as he completed the powerful back-handed swing. Williams staggered back from the table. Colter moved-in with a well-placed right hand to the stomach, followed swiftly with a high left hand to Joey's nose and mouth. Joey hit the floor and lay there motionless.

Ed Baylor stood and went over to Joey, saying, "Joey, you're nothin' but a shit. Ya' can't drink and ya' don't know how to play cards. Ya' don't know nothin', ya' shit!"

Colter sat down and was reaching for the cards. Wade shook his head, saying, "I guess this is as good a time as any to call it a night. It is time I was packin' it in."

"Hell, don't run off, Winchester Man," Colter beamed at Wade, "We usually have to kick the shit outta' him 'jes to get his attention. Most of our damned cows are smarter than him, although not half as dangerous.

"I've had it for the night," said Burney, who picked up the few coins he had left, "Let's get back to the ranch."

"I guess you're right, let's fold 'er up and head out," agreed Colter. He looked at Wade, "How long you goin' to be around town?"

"Probably another day or two before I finish my business here. Why?"

Colter smiled a broad smile At Wade, "'Jes thought I'd take some of your money tomorrow night. We always need new blood aroun' the table." With that Colter swooped up his winnings, and then he and Ed picked Joey up by the armpits and dragged him out of the saloon. As he cleared the front door, he called out, "Adios Murphy!"

Wade could hear the cowhands mounting up outside, amid their curses and oaths to Joey that he had better mount his horse and act like a man. He moved from the poker table back to the bar, shaking his head as he went, "You were right, Mike, that's a bad bunch a' boys."

"You were damned lucky Joey didn't turn on you," Murphy exclaimed, "He can't hold his liquor and he ain't got the sense he was born with. He's drawn down on a number of strangers in here. I don't let him play cards with anyone but the boys he works with. They seem to know how to handle him. Them boys was right, Joey's dumb – but dangerous!"

In his room the following morning, Wade had lathered his face and was putting the straight razor to his beard. He whisked away a day's growth in long easy strokes of the razor. As he shaved under his nose, his thoughts were of what he should do today. First, he had to telegraph Sam Miller's Winchester order to his office in San Francisco; then, he wanted to reconnoiter "Two Dog's" place and do it unseen.

He had a hunch Tate would taking some action soon, and he knew he should be there when it happened. He wanted to be present, but unseen. He'd best learn the lay of Ben's ranch and the time for that was now – today!

Wade left his room walked down the stairs to breakfast. As he came down the stairs, Betty Chalmers looked up from the hotel desk – she smiled and said "Good Morning Mr. Dellums, I trust you slept well."

"Well, Good Morning to you, Mrs. Chalmers. It's a fine day and you're right. I did sleep well, thank you." Wade felt chipper and his mood showed it. "Folks around here tell me you serve the best breakfast in town, is that true?"

"We sure do, Mr. Dellums," she beamed, "We try our darnedest to serve the best. You try it, you'll like it!"

Wade smiled his most charming smile, put his hand to his hat and bowed slightly, saying,"Well, then, that's exactly what I'm goin' to do." With a flourish, he walked into the dining room and took a seat at a small table near the window, so he could watch the activity outside as White Willow was coming awake this Tuesday morning.

As he was finishing a generous plate of eggs and sausage, he felt a large hard hand on his shoulder. He looked up to see Sam Miller standing there. "Good Mornin' Sam. How're you this fine mornin'?"

"Not bad, Wade. Mind if I sit?" Miller asked, as he pulled a chair from under the table.

""You sit yourself right down there, Sam"

"I figured you'd be pulled out of White Willow by now"

"I'm not leaving until I have your order telegraphed to San Francisco, and they've wired me back the order confirmation and a shipping date. That's what I promised, Sam, wasn't it?"

"I guess it was. It's good to see a man who keeps his word. Far too many folks these days will take your order and your money. Then you wait you wait and wait for the merchandise. We're damned careful who we pay first these days. Folks don't seem as honest as they were before the war, ya' know!"

"I've heard that before, Sam," Wade said thoughtfully, "In fact, one person told me he thought it had to do with the migration of displaced Southerners, who lost everything in the war. I don't hold to that – Hell, I've met an awful lot of Northerners – ya' know, the carpetbaggers with their pretty valises and fancy suits. They're all fast talkers and, most of them, I wouldn't trust as far as I could throw my mule, Marybelle!"

Sam's breakfast came and Wade sat with him, talking and sipping his coffee. Wade thought the hot coffee smelled and tasted delicious this morning.

When Miller had finished his breakfast, He and Wade paid the bill and left the dining room. Sam started to cross the street. Wade hung back for a moment, and said, "Sam, I guess I'll leave you for now - got to run down to the telegraph office. I enjoyed the breakfast. I'll see you when they wire back the answer."

"You do that, Wade. I enjoy talkin' with ya'. I'll see ya' later," he waved and walked across the street to his store.

Wade turned to his right and walked down the street toward the telegraph office.

Chapter 6

Wade read the painted lettering on the door. "Telegraph Office, Chilton Travers, Chief Telegrapher." He opened the door and stepped inside.

At the sound of the door, the older man sitting at the desk looked up over his spectacles, and eyed Wade as he stood at the counter. The man was of a light build, gaunt looking and appeared to be in his mid-fifties. He rose and approached the counter.

"Howdy," he said, "What can I do for you today?"

"Howdy, I'd like to send a telegram to my company in San Francisco."

"Well, I reckon we can handle that, Mr. --?"

"Oh, name's Dellums, Wade Dellums. I sell Winchester rifles."

"Glad to know ya', Dellums. Name's Chilton Travers, but most folks 'jes call me Chili. A silly nickname that 'jes seemed to stick to me over the years."

Travers pushed forward a small pad of paper, stating, "Just fill in the name and address – then, down here write in the message. We'll have it along the wire in no time."

"Well, thank you, Mr. Trav – uh, Chili." Wade took up the pencil and wrote the name of the company in San Francisco – Liddle & Kaeding, Post Street, San Francisco. Next, he proceeded with Sam's order and the details of the sale. When he had appurtenants, he added a final line - - Please confirm order, advise earliest possible shipping date – longtime customer needs merchandise earliest – Dellums.

Chili Travers took the pad, counted the words and advised Wade of the price. Wade took some coins from his vest and gave them to Chili, saying, "It'll probably take 'til tomorrow morning for the answer to come back. I've wired them like this before. I'll see you in the mornin', Chili."

"Thank you, Dellums. See ya' in the mornin.'"

He left the telegraph office and walked to the corner where he turned left, heading for the livery stables and Amos Hart.

Wade was concerned about getting his horse out of the stable and having it available, unnoticed - should any trouble start at "Two Dog's" place. And, he didn't want anyone suspecting him of any sort of involvement. By the time he reached the stables, he had a plan forming in his mind.

"Howdy, Amos," he said as he walked into the stables, "How's my girls doin'?"

"Hell, Dellums, they're doin' 'jes great. In fact, 'Ol Marybelle's been quite a lady. Had no trouble with her at all," Amos beamed proudly.

"Great, I'm glad to hear that. Say, Amos, I'm goin' to take Lightfoot over to the blacksmith's – want 'im to check her shoes, then I think I'll ride her some. She needs the exercise and I guess I do too. Bein' aroun' town kinda' gets to me. Maybe a little exercise will do us both good. What do you think?"

"I know what you mean about bein' aroun' town. If I was smart, I'd sell this livery and set out and do some prospectin'," confessed Amos, "I'm too close to the business here, livin' in the back like I do. I need some excitement in my life."

"I hear what you're saying, Amos," Wade returned, as he hefted his saddle and tack and headed for Lightfoot's stall. He put the saddle on the stall door and, in moments, had Lightfoot's headstall on. Next, he placed the blanket on the horse's back, smoothing it and getting it into the proper position. Gently, he lowered the saddle down on the blanket pad, moving it about until it too, was properly placed. With the stirrups hooked on the saddlehorn, Wade reached under Lightfoot's belly, grabbing the cinch and the straps of latigo. He worked the latigo straps into the cinch, securing the saddle to the horse. Then he loosened them. Telling Amos,"Guess I won't tighten them until we are ready to ride – after the shoeing."

Amos nodded in agreement; saying"I can see you take good care of your animals, Wade. I like to see that in a man. Means a lot to the animals, too."

Wade lowered the stirrups and checked the fastening. He put the breastplate on, checking the fastenings again. When he was ready, he led Lightfoot from the stall and out the big door. Standing outside, Wade noticed, for the first time, a large canvass-covered object to his right. He assumed it was a wagon of some type, for he could see wheels showing near the bottom of the canvass.

"Whatcha' got under the canvass, Amos?" Wade asked looking back at Amos.

"That's my pride and joy. Would ya' like to see 'er?"

"If you want to show it to me, then I definitely want to see it, Amos."

Amos moved to the canvass, slowly pulling it away. Slowly, a wagon – no – a surrey emerged from undercover. It was a highly polished black surrey with a yellow fringe along the top. Both leather seats had stuffed cushioning and gleamed in the morning sunlight. It also had two kerosene running lights that glistened along with the rest of the metalwork. The bright sun light gave the surrey an unreal look in a town that was mostly dust and dirt.

"I'd guess you could say this 'ol surrey is the excitement of my life. I've had 'er many years and have cared for 'er dearly. I take her out only for special occasions, like the Fourth of July parade and the Founder's Day rodeo. The rest of the time, I keep 'er cleaned and polished and under the canvass. In a way, it's been a friend for many years. It sounds a bit loco, but it's the way I feel. How do you like 'er, Wade?"

"It's, - it's," Wade stammered, surprised at the beauty of the little rig. "It's a wonder, Amos, it's beautiful," were the words Wade finally found to describe the surrey. The surrey was all of that and then some. It was nearly a work of art. It was easy to see the care Amos had lavished on it over the years. Everything was clean and shiny just like the day, many years ago, when the surrey was manufactured in some Eastern buggyworks.

"I'm glad you appreciate 'er for what she is, Wade," Amos smirked, adding, "She's right purty, ain't she?"

"She's a beauty, Amos, and I can see why you keep 'er covered. How long you had it?"

"I got 'er right after the War. Bought it from a Yankee salesman, who was down on his luck and needed some cash to get back East. It was new then. I'd say I've had it for eighteen – nineteen years at least. Wouldn't know it to look at 'er, would ya'?"

"She looks to be brand new," Wade assured, then leading Lightfoot by the reins, he said, "thank you for showing me your pride and joy. You should be right proud."

"That I am – that I am, see ya' later, Dellums."

Wade waved to Amos and led the horse to the corner and turned left to the end of the street, where the blacksmith kept his shop

No one seemed to pay much attention to their presence as he and Lightfoot walked along the street. He certainly hoped he could continue his image as a quiet, unassuming rifle salesman – the man everyone seemed to like, and the man no one paid any particular attention to.

The sign over the door read, "Grant's Smithy, Tom Bartlett, Prop." Wade walked to the open door and peered inside, where a good-sized man about Wade's age, was working at the forge. He was shaping some shoes – working the red hot shoe in the coals of the forge. He moved the shoe from the coals to the anvil; where he hit it with a heavy hammer, shaping the shoe the way he wanted it. Wade waited until the shoe was back in the forge, then he called out,"Good Mornin'"

The smithy turned and acknowledged

Wade's presence, then he turned back to the forge, releasing the shoe and placing the tongs and hammer on the anvil.

"Good Morn' what can I do for you?" he asked.

"Lightfoot here, needs some new shoes. I think her right front shoe is loose, too. Thought maybe you could take a look at 'em."

"Be glad to, bring 'er inside. Name's Bartlett, Tom Bartlett," he offered his hand in greeting.

"Glad to know you, Tom. My name's Wade Dellums. I'm down from Missoula way."

"Are you here visitin'?"

"Naw, I'm a salesman – sell Winchester rifles for an outfit out of San Francisco. I'm here to see Sam Miller."

"Well, Welcome to White Willow."

Bartlett moved-in and raised each of the horse's hooves, checking each thoroughly. Wade watched as Bartlett moved about the horse – he wasted no moves, each an efficient and gentle one. Lightfoot stood quietly. Bartlett's gentleness calmed her. It was easy to see Tom Bartlett had spent much of his life around animals - horses, in particular.

"You have a way with horses, Tom. I've never seen Lighfoot so calm, with someone checkin' out her hooves."

"Not much to it, really – you just remain calm and assure her that everything is alright. I guess they sense I care and won't hurt them. He stood and approached Wade, "She can use some shoes. Hooves need trimming some, too."

"Well, better get her some new shoes then. How long a job is that, Tom?"

"It shouldn't take too long. I gotta' set of shoes in the forge that should fit 'er. Probably take an hour or so. That alright with you?"

"That's great, Tom. Afterwards, I think I'll take a little ride. I thought I'd head towards Salmon. Went through there in the dark the other night. I probably could sell some rifles there.

"I'm originally from Salmon. Been here since '75, when I bought this place from Ed Grant. I was born and raised in Salmon, where I learned this trade at my father's forge and anvil."

'Salmon's a pretty nice town. How come you left there?"

"I wanted a place of my own. Dad's still there – gotta' a good little business. When Ed Grant got a hankerin' to go to California, I came down and bought this place. I married a local girl – she's the daughter of the telegrapher here. Mary's six month pregnant – so, I'd guess you'd say I have my roots here now."

"Sounds like you're doin' great, Tom." Wade turned toward the door, saying, "I'll be back in an hour or so."

Walking back to the hotel, he explored the situation – to see if the plan would work. His horse is free of the livery stable. Amos has no suspicions as to why and Bartlett knows he's riding north.

He could now ride out and check "TwoDog's" spread. His basic plan called for riding out unobserved to 'Two Dog's" to check the lay of the land. Once there, and after checking the terrain – he'd have to devise a plan to counter any action Charlie Tate and his boys might take.

The plan dictated he'd have to get back to town unnoticed, and be visible around town this afternoon and evening. He'd have to appear as though he'd been around town all day.

Wade knew approximately where "Two Dogs'" was located. As the crow flies, that is. Sam Miller had waved his hand in the direction, when he briefly mentioned Ben and his problem with Tate. The ranch lay north and west of town on the other side of the Lemhi Mountain Range. The mountains were directly west of town. In the distance, Wade could se a good-sized pass that lay south of White Willow, a well-worn trail leading to it. However, further north along the range, was a mountain saddle that might be passable. It appeared to offer good cover for a horse and rider, what with the many trees and rocks, boulders actually, that lined the approach to the saddle. It might be possible to get up and over and back again without being seen.

He planned to ride north later, as if heading for Salmon, then work around to the west when he was out of sight of the town. If all goes well, he will be able to check out the mountain saddle and no one would be the wiser. He decided to go with the plan and refine it as he goes.

He returned to his hotel room, where he had further details to add to his plan. *First,* he thought, *I'll need a rifle.* Wade selected one of the demonstration carbines; in fact, the one he and Sam Miller had fired during the demonstration down in the wash. If suspicions came his way, he could state that both he and Sam had fired the arm recently.

Next – it was likely he and Lightfoot would pick up some trail dust, and to come into town covered with dust could be a dead giveaway. He grabbed his trail clothes, a brush for the horse and a clean piece of rag – the kind he used to clean the Winchesters with. He put the carbine – it was a Winchester, .45-.60, the clothes and other items in the leather satchel he used as his sales valise. He could carry the satchel in and out of the hotel without raising any eyebrows. He'd look like what he was, a Winchester salesman carrying his wares. He also threw in some cartridges for the .45-.60.

He lay on his bed for a while, thinking about what he was about to do. As far as he could tell there were no kinks in his plan. At nine a.m. he rose, gathered up his sales satchel and headed for Tom Bartlett's.

Chapter 7

Stepping down the stairs to the hotel lobby, Wade was pleased to see that Betty Chalmers wasn't standing at her desk. He walked through the lobby area and out the door, casually but promptly, turned right and walked toward Tom Bartlett's place.

Lightfoot was standing outside, tied to a hitching post. He could see the new shoes. Great, he thought, now I can get moving. Tom came out and told Wade the price for his services. – "That'll be two dollars, Wade."

"I hope Lightfoot didn't give you any trouble, Tom," he said as he handed Tom the money.

"Naw, she was as helpful as a horse can be. Guess she wanted new shoes, too."

Wade tied the leather satchel to the back of his saddle, securing it with rawhide strings. "I guess we'll go and try them out. What do ya' say, Lightfoot?" He tightened down the latigo straps and stepped up onto the saddle. "Thanks, Tom. See ya 'later." And he rode out of town.

After he had ridden for about twenty minutes, he came to a wide wash – a channel cut into the prairie floor that handled the spring rain runoff from the mountains. It was dry this time of the year. He rode into the wash and found he couldn't see White Willow - nor, could anyone see him. Wade followed it for a while, then he stopped and stepped down. He removed his town clothes and put on his trail outfit. After he placed the town clothes in the satchel, he remounted and reined Lightfoot to the west, toward the mountains.

Before long, the terrain began to rise and gain elevation. He kept looking back toward town, assuring himself he was moving unseen. He started up the approach to the saddle. He rode carefully, making sure the trees and boulders were between him and the view from town. He could tell this saddle was little used as a mountain crossing. It was steep and narrow, far too narrow for a wagon or a buggy. Nearing the top, the faint trail narrowed even more, but it was wide enough for Lightfoot to move through. Luckily it was early fall and no snow had fallen as yet. Good, thought Wade, there'll be no snow tracks to worry about.

When he was through the saddle – actually, it was a small pass and being narrow, folks preferred to use the wider and lower pass to the south. He rode downgrade for a short time, and then he reined-in. He stepped down, deciding to let Lightfoot rest a bit. Tying the horse short to a tree, he scouted around some – looking for a promontory from which he could look down into the valley below. He found a large outcropping that would serve his purpose. He laid flat on the rock, letting his eyes search the valley.

About a mile south, he noticed a fence line. Barbed wire indicated the presence of Man. He followed the line of the fence, tracing the shape with his eyes. He could make out pastures enclosed by fences. If Sam Miller had pointed in the right direction, Wade reasoned, this had to be Ben's place.

However, he couldn't see a ranch house. Where would I put a house if it were my place? he asked his mind. He thought it over, deciding he'd put house in the foothills above the pastures, out of the wind and near a good water source – perhaps a mountain spring. He decided the reason he couldn't see the house was because the trees and boulders that lay in between, blocked his line of sight. "So far, so good," he murmured as he walked back to his horse.

He walked the horse, keeping quiet and unseen. He picked his way carefully for about a half a mile, when he discovered a natural overhang that reached out and touched the nearby trees. He stopped here. *This would good cover for Lightfoot,* he thought, tying the horse securely to a tree. There was some vegetation she could nibble at. Nothing with much nourishment, but it would keep her occupied while he was scouting the mountainside.

He picked his way carefully through the trees, rocks and boulders. The boulders here were quite large and afforded good cover. In a while, he could make out the shapes of some buildings below, located a little further south of his present position. He continued south until he could make out the house and barn clearly.

Wade returned to his horse where he checked the reins again to see if they were tied securely. He didn't want Lightfoot wandering off. He gave her an affectionate pat on the flanks to reassure her. The horse looked back at him, as if to say, "I am fine – hurry back." He walked out about thirty yards and looked back to see if Lightfoot's cover was good. With the shadow from the overhang and the trees, he could barely make out that there was a horse tied there. *Great,* he thought, *now let's get down to business.*

Moving from boulder to boulder, Wade worked his way to a position directly above the house. The boulders here, he noted, were very large, providing plenty of cover for a man to hide behind. From this position, there was an excellent view of the house, corral and barn. He could see a man pitching hay into a wagon. He also saw a young boy of five or six playing on the porch of the house. Scanning the whole area, Wade couldn't see any dogs. Good, he smiled; a dog could sense a man's presence and give away his position.

Wade lay there quietly for a long time, scanning the terrain all around him. He looked far out in the distance, where he could see cattle grazing – then his eyes traced a line up the grade to the gate and fence that led to the house and barn. Next, he looked out to the trail that led to the ranch. It ran straight west out of the gate and turned to a southerly direction. That's the direction Tate would come from, he decided.

He turned and looked up, checking his back to see if anyone could get behind him. He also checked to see if there might be an escape route should he run into trouble. The mountain grew quite steep, and he'd have to climb to get out that way. He decided his back was well-covered and he'd have to leave the way he came in.

He got a better view of the man working below near the barn. Damn, Wade realized, I don't know him. Now he was uncertain about whose ranch this might be. A man came out of the house and walked to the barn. It was Ben Taylor – his buddy, "Two Dogs." He did have the right place after all. The man at the barn must be a hired hand – he looks much older than Ben. The older man came out to meet Ben and they talked near the corral. As they talked, Ben kept pointing to the pasture down below.

Shortly, a woman came out of the house and motioned to the two men. Wade could see she was young and very attractive. He smiled, thinking; leave it Ben to have a pretty lady!

She motioned again as the young boy came to her side. The men waved and came to the house. Wade looked at the slight shadows then looked up to the sun. Must be near noon – dinner time. That's what they are doin', going in to eat. *Great,* he thought, *now I can move around a little up here and find me the best position. I need a spot that's closer where I can see all of the house, barn and yard.*

He spotted a huge boulder a little downgrade from his position. There was a tree at a lower elevation that would cover his movement to the boulder. He moved down and from this position he could see it all. He figured he was less than one hundred and fifty feet from the yard. This'll be my position, he decided, good cover all the way around. He lay quiet for a few moments, realizing the next time he came to this spot – he'd have to bring some branches to use to wipe out his tracks in the dust. He'd cut the branches a mile or so back so the cutting wouldn't be noticed near the ranch.

Wade quickly made his way back to the horse, untied her reins and walked Lightfoot back the way they'd come earlier. When they had walked about a half of a mile, he mounted

Lightfoot and rode quietly up through the saddle and down the other side into the wash. He rode slowly along the wash, looking for a place to hide his satchel. He found a good place. It was a heavy bush that could conceal the satchel.

He stepped down and untied the leather satchel, taking the clean cloth and brush from it. He cleaned and brushed Lightfoot, removing all traces of dust and sweat. When the horse looked presentable, he removed his town clothes from the satchel and brushed them thoroughly – Damn, black was a bad color to make dust-free. He worked a long time on his black hat.

When everything looked acceptable, Wade changed into his town clothes, putting the dusty trail clothes in the satchel. He dug a hole and with the aid of a rock for ballast, he secured the bush over the satchel. The carbine went into the holster on the saddle with the extra cartridges thrown into the saddlebags.

He checked both himself and the horse for the last time. Satisfied, he mounted and rode slowly to town. As he rode, he worked on his plan. So far, so good! If I get lucky, I'll be in my covered position when Tate and his boys show up at "Two Dog's". "Probably take more'n luck," he whispered to the wind.

Back in town as he rode past the blacksmith's, Tom Bartlett called out, "I thought you were goin' up Salmon?"

"I changed my mind – decided to stop there when I head back to Montana. We had a good ride though. Lightfoot says to tell you she likes her new shoes." Wade smiled and said, "Thanks again, Tom."

Walking up the main street, Wade looked for a good place to leave Lightfoot. It had to be someplace not too conspicuous – some place a standing, saddled horse would look natural. He chose the side street. The street headed west and was in front, but off to the side of Chalmer's Saloon. He reined in, stepped down and tied the horse to the rail. He patted the horse a bit, and then he loosened the latigo straps. "Have some patience, 'Ol Girl", he whispered into her ear. Lightfoot whinnied as if she understood.

Wade looked up at the sun – it appeared to be about two in the afternoon. It had taken him nearly three hours to reconnoiter Ben's place. I could get back here in three quarters of an hour, if I had to his logic said. I'll probably have to when the time comes. He walked into Chalmer's Saloon.

"Howdy Ned, how are you today?" Wade offered quietly as he stepped up to the long walnut-finished bar.

"Just fine, Mr. Dellums," Ned returned.

"Wade, call me Wade, Ned."

"Sorry Wade, what'll you have," he asked, "The same?'

"Whiskey's fine, thank you."

Ned poured the shot, and asked, "How's the Winchester business goin'?"

"Fine! – Great actually! Sam Miller bought a good supply of them. We went out to the wash outside of town. Ya' know, the one folks use for shootin' practice? Sam fired the new Model '86 for a while. I could tell he was pleased as punch about the new Winchesters. He placed a good order. Fact is, I'm waiting for my firm in San Francisco to telegraph me the confirmation of the order and the shipping date. That way, Sam'll know when the order should arrive."

"Good," Ned beamed, "Now I can start workin' on Elizabeth – that's her real name, ya' know – Betty's a nickname. Anyhow, I gotta' work on her a little, so's I can get one of the first new Winchesters when they get here. Like I said before, she controls the purse strings."

"She's a nice lady, Ned. I know she's been nice to me since I've been here."

"She's a nice person, no doubt about that. She said she thought you were a gentleman. I think she likes you, young fella'."

Wade smiled, lifted his glass and toasted Ned.

Wade had another drink, talking with Ned until close to five o'clock – then he went upstairs to wash for supper.

Chapter 8

Stepping out of the hotel, Wade looked down the way to Murphy's Saloon. There were only two horses tied up in front of the place. Not much of an early evening crowd on Tuesday nights, he calculated. Probably too early for Charlie Tate's boys, he thought. Damn, I hope they're coming to town tonight. Hmm, what to do? I've got to kill some time, besides its too early for a drink, what with supper sitting full on my stomach.

He turned to his right and noticed a barber's pole. The barber shop was located next to the telegraph office. That's the place to go, he thought, besides I need a haircut. Who know I might learn something sitting in the barber's chair. Damn, I hope I'm not too late.

"Howdy, hope I'm not too late – been needin' a haircut bad."

"Howdy," the barber said, "I was plannin' on go home but I guess one more won't hurt me."

"Thanks, I appreciate that," Wade said, removing his hat and hanging it on a heavy peg on the wall. He was looking for a place to sit, when an older man – his haircut finished, got up from the barber's chair. Wade sat down on the chair as the older man paid the barber, found his hat, and said, "see ya' next time, Wil."

The barber turned, shook the hair from his barber's cape, turned again and in one motion, twirled the cape over Wade's head. It settled on Wade's lap easily. The barber was securing the cape at the back of Wade's neck, as he said, "Truth is, I don't that many customers that I can afford to turn one away."

'Well. I appreciate it. I should have thought about a haircut this afternoon. Seems I tend to forget about something I can't see directly, if you catch what I mean?"

"Yeh, I do – a lot of folks are that way. They wait until they look like sheep dogs. They come in with an apology, always. It's a standing joke with barbers, but that's the way folks are. Damned hard to change 'em. You're new around here, ain't cha'?"

"Yep, I travel a lot – a salesman – I sell Winchester rifles and carbines. My name's Dellums, Wade Dellums," said Wade, offering his hand from under the cape.

The barber switched his comb and scissors to his left hand. With his right he shook Wade's hand with a hearty handshake. "Glad to meet ya", Dellums. I'm Wil Grant."

"Glad to know ya' Wil," Wade said, as he returned his hand to his side, underneath the cape.

"I saw you go by earlier today. You looked liked you were on the way to the telegraph office next door."

"You are right on the button," Wade laughed, "that's where I was headin' – to send a telegram."

Well, you have to excuse me, Wade, but when I spend all day standin' here, cutting hair and looking out the window – you see everything and everyone who goes by. Just a habit, I guess, it helps the time go by."

"No offense taken, Wil," Wade soothed, "I've been calling on Sam Miller – showing him the new Model '86 Winchesters. He gave me a good order. That's a good man, that Sam Miller."

Sam Miller is a good man. He keeps a good store too," Grant assured, his hands moving swiftly about Wade's head – the comb and scissors working in concert – small snips of hair falling on the cape.

Wade asked Wil Grant about the tooth that hung outside, next to the barber pole. "I see by the tooth hanging out there, you must be the town dentist?"

"Wal, not really. I'm the town puller. I'd guess that's the best way to say it. I'm not a dentist. I just pull teeth that are hurtin'. Extractions, they call them in San Francisco. In White Willow, I call it pulling – 'cause that is what it takes to get a damned tooth out, a lot of tugging and pulling!"

"I've seen a lot of barber shops aroun' the West that pull teeth too. – Quite often, the sign says "Tonsorial Parlor.""

"That's just a funny name for what I do here. The striped pole and the tooth say the same thing. I imagine barbers pull teeth because the barber's chair resembles the dentist's chair. I sent away to San Francisco for the tooth hanging out there and some fancy tools for pulling teeth. Just fancy pliers, is all they are."

"That makes sense to me," agreed Wade, watching the progress of his haircut in the mirror to his front.

Wil Grant continued his clipping and combing for a time. Finally, he asked Wade what it was like traveling around, moving from town-to-town. Wade explained. "That it was fun and exciting at the beginning - but, after a while, it has become wearying work. Always leaving a town – always coming to a town. Every hotel room seemed much like the last one – dull, drab and devoid of personality, of warmth and friendliness."

"Once in a while, Wade further explained, "You come to a town like White Willow and you feel glad you travel. You feel glad that you got here, 'cause in White Willow the folks are friendly, the hotel room is comfortable – even the meals are home-cooked and tasty. Like most everything, travel has its good sides and bad sides, I guess."

"I guess I never thought of it that way, Dellums," Grant said thoughtfully, "there must something to the old saying, and "The grass is always greener on the other side of the fence."

"Tell me, feeling as you do about traveling, you planning on doin' it for long?"

"Lately, I have to admit, the thought of settling down comes to mind a lot – particularly when I'm on the trail between towns."

"I guess it would be on the trail –Say, lookee there!' Wil blurted out, as he swung Wade's to face the window. "See those three? Those boys are trouble! Probably heading for Murphy's Saloon. Some of Charlie Tate's hands. They come in at night and on Saturdays and get all liquored up. Most folks give them a wide berth, if you know what I mean."

Wade watched as the three riders passed by the window. *Good,* Wade thought to himself, *those are the three from the camp that night. Maybe I'm in luck tonight?* He looked up at Wil Grant and said, "Every town has its bad characters – I guess that's what makes White Willow normal, doesn't it?"

"Wal, this town would be better off if they weren't around, I can tell you that."

Wade noticed the light from the late afternoon was nearly gone, the shop growing darker by the minute. The barber was putting the finishing touches to Wade's hair. Wade figured Grant didn't want to light a lamp for fear of another customer wanting a late-hour, much needed, haircut.

When the barber turned his chair to face the mirror Wade could barely see his reflected image. Grant was loosening the cape. "Looks great, Wil," Wade complimented, "makes me look human again."

"I'm glad you stopped in, Wade. It was good talkin' with you. Maybe now I'll think twice about travelin' when I get bored looking out of my window here."

Wade handed him a silver dollar, said thanks again and they shook hands. "See you the next time you come to town. You'll probably need a haircut bad." Grant smirked, as Wade laughed and walked out of the shop.

-- - - - -

The sun had dropped into the Western horizon, leaving dark, rough shadows in the large ranch house. Charlie Tate was busy lighting a number of lamps around the room. The room served as Tate's office. It was a large room located off the sitting room.

An immense desk dominated the room. A tall, leather-cushioned chair sat behind the desk; all the other chairs in the room – there were six of them – were hard straight-backed chairs built for utility, not comfort . . . and that was the way Charlie Tate wanted it. When you sat before his desk, he didn't want you comfortable; he wanted you uncomfortable, uneasy and willing to give in to whatever his wishes were. Tate's main thrust in life and business – was to intimidate and dominate to get his way. That was the way of the man!

Charlie finished the lamps and sat down behind his desk, going over some of the many papers strewn across its surface. He sat back abruptly, reached into a drawer, took out a large cigar and looked around for a match. Having no luck in his search, he got up and went across the room to the fireplace, where a supply of wooden matches was kept. He grabbed a handful and returned to the desk where he opened a drawer and threw the matches in it. Taking one match, he dragged it across the desktop. When it ignited, he directed the flame to the end of his cigar. He puffed a couple of times, drawing full to get the volume of smoke he required. He took the cigar from his mouth and looked at the lighted red embers. Satisfied the cigar was lit the way he liked it; he growled," Good!"

Charlie Tate wasn't happy and his face showed it!

Moments later, the door opened and his ranch foreman, Matt Weber, walked in. "How are you tonight, Charlie?" he asked as he stepped into the room.

Charlie looked up from his desk. His eyes narrowed and he bellowed, "Mad as hell – sit down!" He leaned back in his chair, drawing full on his cigar. "Tell me Slick, what you found out about those ready-made saddles? What did 'Ol Man Miller have to say?"

Slick Weber squirmed for a moment – *Damn, how he hated sittin' in these straight-backed chairs.* He comforted himself as best he could and said, "I talked with Miller this afternoon and he said the saddles are on the trail, comin' in from Idaho Falls. Should be here tomorrow or the next day – the latest. Miller said he had learned that from the telegram he sent. He said he then wired Idaho Falls to check out where the saddles were exactly. That's when they told him the saddles were on the trail. Shit, I believe 'im, Charlie." he finished.

"They had better show up in the next couple of days or, Screw 'em! - I cancel the order."

"What else did you learn in town today?"

"Ted's wire was there. He left Idaho Falls today. He'll be here as soon as he can."

"So Ted Pettibone's finally got his ass in the saddle. Damned attorney should have been here a week ago. I s'pose that damned crook had to screw a few more of the good citizens of Idaho Falls before he could ride out. Well, good," Charlie smiled for the first time, "Now let's talk about some business we gotta' do."

Weber shifted again, trying for more comfort and not finding it. "What sort of business do you have in mind, Charlie?"

Tate leaned back in his chair, holding his cigar up, appraising it as he slowly turned it in his had. "It's time we settled Mr. Ben "Two Dogs" Taylor's hash. I mean to get that damned ranch and I mean to get it now."

"Do you have a plan, Charlie?"

"Damned right, I do. We're ridin' over there in the mornin' – early – and he's goin' to sign these papers. Oh, he'll sign 'em, or I'll beat it out of 'im! These papers gotta' be signed by the time Pettibone gets here. He needs signed papers so he can file them all legal-like."

"Shit, Charlie, you know Taylor's not goin' to sign willingly. He's told you enough times that he ain't goin' to sell out his place. We'll have to make him sign at gunpoint."

"I don't care how we make 'im do it. We'll run off the stock again, if we have to we'll burn the house and barn.

"Ah'll send 'im packing, that's f'sure . . . And he will sign these papers."

"Wal, you're the boss, Charlie. Whatever you say, we'll do, that's f'sure."

"Ya' got that damned right, Slick," Tate roared at his foreman. "We ride at first light, ya' got that? I want ya' to take all the boys. The more the merrier, I always say. They ought to scare the shit outta' Mr. Ben "Two Dogs" Taylor."

"Yeh, six of us standin' there ought to get Taylor's attention – not to mention his pretty little wife," Slick Weber smiled with a menacing grin.

"We got no truck with the woman, Slick," Tate bellowed, "I 'jes want these papers and that's all. Ya' got that?"

"I got it, Boss," Weber said in a not too convincing tone.

"Are all the boys on the ranch tonight?" Charlie asked.

"Naw, Joey's here, but Mike, Ed and Bill rode into town – probably to play cards at Murphy's."

"Damn, I want to ride at first light! Slick, you ride in and get those boys back here. I don't want any drunks in the mornin' Ya' hear? Get 'em and get 'em now, 'cause we ride at first light – sober!"

"I got it, Charlie. I'll go after 'em. See ya' in the mornin' – sober." Slick Weber got up from the chair and headed for his horse. "Damn," he muttered under his breath, "I need a night ride to town like I need a hole in my head."

Chapter 9

Wade was back in his hotel room, busying himself around the room. He opened the bed and laid on it for a while. He wanted the bed to look slept in. There was an off-hand chance he wouldn't be sleeping in the bed tonight. His gut instincts told him it was time for Tate to move on Ben. He hoped that he'd learn something from Tate's cowhands tonight that would send him to his hideaway position above "Two Dog's" ranch house. *If only my luck holds out,* he thought.

Checking his pockets, Wade couldn't find his jackknife. Where did the knife get to? He looked in his saddlebags and found it. The knife would be needed for cutting a bushy branch to wipe out his tracks in the dust. There were plenty of cartridges for the Winchester. Actually, Wade had told Sam Miller a little white lie about not having anymore of the new smokeless cartridges. There were plenty of them in the saddlebags. His Colt.44 revolver was loaded, but the cartridge belt was partially empty. Methodically, he pushed the cartridges into the open spaces on the belt, filling the belt full.

Next, he moved around the room, making it look like it looked every morning. He washed and left the wet soap on the stand, a wet towel next to it. He put some clothes on the floor, some over the back of a chair. He knew Betty Chalmers didn't do the rooms until early afternoon. By then, she'd have seen him around the hotel and he knew she'd have no questions where he was the night before – sleeping in his room, of course.

It's time, he realized. The streets were dark now and he judged the time to be about nine o'clock. Best he get down to Murphy's and see what Tate's cowhands are up to.

Wade had felt a chill in the air when he left the barber shop earlier. *Fall is settlin' in,* he thought at the time. With that in mind, he reached for his denim jacket and slipped it on. He looked himself over in the mirror, decided he was ready and left the room.

Coming down the hotel stairs, he noticed Betty Chalmers was not at her front desk. Probably in their living quarters behind the lobby area, he guessed. He stepped outside and walked quickly to Murphy's Saloon.

Coming in through the barroom doors, Wade spotted the Tate cowhands standing at the bar. Walking over to the bar, Wade said, "Howdy Boys, could ya' stand a drink?"

They turned as a group and smiled. Bill Colter, who was the closest to Wade said, "Does a bear shit in the buckwheat?"

Wade smiled and looked at Murphy, "Mike, give these boys a drink."

While Murphy was pouring the whiskey, Wade leaned into the bar and looked at the trio, "You boys been up to anythin' good?"

"Shit No," Colter responded, "'jes chasin' Tate's critters and mendin' fences."

"You boys come to town to try and get the rest of my money?" Wade challenged, alluding to last night's poker game.

Mike Burney, who was standing in the middle, leaned in and said,"Ya' know Dellums, the thought had crossed our minds."

"Yeh," Colter laughed, "like I said, we dearly love new blood, particularly so close to payday."

"I think you boys are trying to pluck a mighty skinny goose, but I guess I could sit-in a few hands later."

"That's right nice of ya, Winchester Man," Colter beamed. He turned to Mike Murphy, "Mike, better give Mr. Dellums here another drink."

They stood at the bar for several more drinks, bantering back and forth; chiding one another in tones, friendly and not so friendly – typical barroom talk that serves to pass the time on a quiet evening.

After a while, Wade asked where Joey was.

"Ya' mean asshole?" Ed Baylor offered in return, "we left 'im at the ranch. Claimed he was still sore from whuppin' Bill gave 'im last night."

"Truth is," interrupted Colter, "the asshole's broke. Good thing too. Every time we bring 'im to town, he causes some kinda' trouble. The kid's got shit for brains. 'Ol Man Tate likes 'im though - I guess its 'cause Joey'll do anything Tate tells him to do."

"He sure screwed up last night's game, didn't he?" Burney asked.

Wade smiled a thin smile, "Yeh, he did that. Joey is trouble looking for a place to happen."

Colter laughed, "Ya' know, I think you are right, Winchester Man – that's what Joey is – trouble looking for place to happen. I like it. Never heard Joey described any better. Let's have another, Mike."

Mike poured another round of shots, as Mike Burney said, "C'mon Bill, let's play some poker and see how skinny that goose really is."

"Whatta' you say, Dellums? Ya' ready for some poker?" Colter asked.

"You betcha'," Wade said and downed his shot.

They were moving to the poker table when the doors opened and Slick Weber strode in, in a brusque manner. He approached the men who were, by now, pulling out their chairs, ready to sit.

"No poker tonight boys. – ya' gotta' get back to the ranch – Tate's orders. We're ridin' early – sober!"

"Shit, "Burney exclaimed, "Can't that man leave us alone – even at night?"

"Where are we goin' early in the mornin'?" Ed Baylor asked, a not too happy frown on his face.

Weber bristled a little, a rage building that comes from having his orders questioned, "'jes never ya' mind where. Get your ass in the saddle and get on back to the ranch. Tate wants everyone sober in the mornin' - we're ridin' at first light."

Colter turned to Weber and stared for moment, "Christ, you're serious, ain't ya' Slick?"

"You're damned right I am – ya' think I'd ride to town 'jes to shoot bullshit at ya'? Now drink up – I'll be waitin' outside. Let's go boys."

Weber stalked out of the barroom. Weber wasn't happy! Colter looked at Wade with a sort of helpless look, "Damn Tate hires ya' and he thinks he owns ya'."

Wade said nothing, returning Colter's look with an understanding nod.

Mike Burney was furious, He chucked his shot down his throat, "Damn, I know where we're goin' at first light. Taylor's, that where. Shit, I knew it. Damned man'll get us killed, you mark my words. I mean it Colter."

"Shut up Mike. C'mon Ed, drink up and let's get on back. It's best not to keep Slick waitin'," With that Colter started for the door, Baylor and Burney following along reluctantly.

As the door closed behind them – Wade - who was still standing at the poker table smiled, thinking that his luck was still holding. Tomorrow's the day! Good, I'll be there – waiting.

Turning from the table, he headed for the bar. Murphy was standing there in silence after he had taken in the events of the past few moments.

"Ya' know, Wade, I always breathe a sigh of relief when them boys ride out of here."

"Hell, Mike, they don't seem too bad, although I have to admit Joey's a dangerous kid to be around."

"You've never seen them all liquored-up! A couple of months back, Colter shot a man in here. He got away with self-defense. They egged the man on so that he drew on

Colter. Colter nailed 'im right there at the poker table. Claimed self-defense. - The boys backed 'im up, plus a couple of other fella's backed 'im, mostly out of fear. Wasn't much the Sheriff could do."

Two older men came into the bar. Mike went on down the bar to serve them. Wade's mind was racing thinking about what he had to do now. First, he decided, he'd hang around the bar as long as he could. He didn't want to arouse any suspicions connected with the Tate boy's early departure. He'd stay and talk with Mike. Probably should change the subject of our conversation too, he figured.

Murphy returned and changed the subject himself, when he asked, "How long ya' goin' to be in town, Wade?"

"Probably 'til tomorrow, I guess. I'm waiting on a telegram from my company in San Francisco confirming Sam's order – then I'm free to head out."

"Where ya' headin' next?"

"It's funny you should ask, Mike. I was pondering that when you were down the bar before. I really should head south for Idaho Falls, but somethin' inside me says I really ought to get back to my ranch up north in the Bitterroots. I've been on the trail for a long while now. I'd like to spend some time at home."

"I gotcha', Wade, sometimes it's good for a man to get back home and lay back for a time."

Murphy poured another shot, then he and Wade talked for a while. More men came into the bar and Murphy moved back and forth serving them in turn. In those moments when Mike was busy down the bar, Wade's mind worked over each step of his plan for the morning. When he had gone over it a number of times, he decided the plan would work with no problems. If a problem should arise, he felt he could revise and still move ahead with the plan – and, if his luck continued to hold, the plan would work.

Murphy was back and was beginning to talk about his family and how lucky he is the have the wife he has. Mike claimed, "She stuck with me through thick and thin, that she was a religious woman who didn't hold to drinkin' and smokin' In spite of her persuasion, she never said a word when Mike had bought the saloon. He didn't drink or smoke at home, of course. He figured she realized the saloon was a business and a good means to make a living. All in all, it worked out pretty good with her," he concluded.

"You're lucky, Mike. I've never been married and now that I'm in my thirties, I keep thinkin' it might be time for me to settle down – find me a good woman and start working the ranch seriously.

"Well, I'd say there's nothin' like having a family and a home. Best thing there is! It gives a man some roots and somethin to hold on to. Hell, you're not getting any younger ya' know."

"You could be right – yes, you could be right," Wade agreed, after a long, thoughtful pause. He drained his shot glass, and with a slight wave of his hand at Murphy, "I guess it's time for me to pack it in. That 'ol pillow will feel good tonight. I'll stop by tomorrow, Mike, before I leave."

Murphy said good night and Wade stepped out into the cool night. He looked up and saw the waning moon – it looked to be no more than a sliver of what it was a couple of nights before. Good, he realized – he didn't want too much moon light for this night's activities. He has work to do!

Chapter 10

The light was dark and shadowy in the street near Chalmer's Saloon. The saloon was closed for the night. Wade patted Lightfoot affectionately, pulling in the latigo straps to insure the saddle was secure. Untying the reins, he led the horse slowly and quietly down the side street that led west out of town. They walked carefully, making little sound in the still of the night.

Several hundred yards out of town proper, Wade stepped up into the saddle, walking Lightfoot slowly to the north. He looked back occasionally to see if anyone had noticed their departure. There were no lights to be seen and no one had been in the streets. Wade felt he'd managed to slip out of town unnoticed. His next stop was the wash where he'd change his clothes.

Before long the dark line of the wash began to take form in the terrain ahead. He rode into it and went to the west for a bit, looking for the bush that concealed his leather satchel. When he saw it, he stepped down, grabbed up the satchel and then led Lightfoot further down the wash. He was looking for a place he spotted yesterday, a section with a copse of willows along the backs of the wash. It had a good supply of grass for the horse to nibble at. He found the spot, tied Lightfoot with enough rein so she could eat in grass.

Wade removed her saddle and blanket, brushing her back and belly down well. He next flipped the saddle over so that the under-fleece might dry out some. It and the blanket were damp with horse sweat.

With Lightfoot taken care of, Wade brushed his clothes and hat and changed into his trail clothes from the satchel. He folded his town clothes neatly and placed them into the satchel. The Winchester came next. He loaded the carbine with the new smokeless cartridges. He worked the action, allowing several cartridges to fall to the ground. Seeing the cartridges on the ground made him realize that he would have pick up any spent cartridges if he fired in the morning. If I do any firing, I sure don't want anyone to know I was there.

With his last minute preparations completed, he settled down with his back to the wall of the bank. Checking the night sky, he decided it couldn't be much more than midnight. Time to catch some sleep – maybe two or three hours. Wade wanted to be alert at dawn, not drowsy from lack of sleep. He closed his eyes and nodded off.

The next thing his mind heard was Lightfoot munching on the grass close to his ear. His eyes snapped open and he checked the night sky. He calculated he had slept perhaps for four hours. First light can't be far off, he reasoned. It was time to get movin'. Rising, he shook the dust from his clothes. As he saddled the horse, he looked for a good place to cache the satchel. Nearby was an overhang created by some willows that would work well. He hid the satchel, mounted Lightfoot and rode west.

It was still dark when he reached the trees and overhang where he would leave Lightfoot. Stepping down, he secured the reins, leaving enough slack to nibble at what sparse grass there was. He moved into the trees and found a spruce with plenty of limbs and needles. Wade cut a bushy limb from the north side of the tree – figuring it would not be easily noticed by someone coming from the south. Stuffing extra cartridges in his pockets, he removed the carbine from the saddle scabbard and moved off in a low crouch.

When he arrived at the boulder he'd chosen as the best position, he placed the branch and the carbine on the ground and say quietly observing the area below. He could see dim lights in the ranch house. Ah yes, he remembered, ranch life starts early in the morning. It has been a while, he realized, since he had to get up early. This salesman's life is spoiling me, he decided.

The morning light began to brighten far to the west of his position behind the boulder. Fortunately, the mountainside to his rear would help keep this area semi-dark, much longer than the area down below where the cattle were grazing. He felt the subdued light would work to his advantage.

- - - - -

It was still dark when Slick Weber went shouting and stomping through the bunkhouse, waking up the cowhands. He smiled as they grumbled and stumbled to their feet. He wished he had a bugle, remembering his days in the Army. Damn, how he hated bugles!

"Let's go, let's go! Up and at 'em! Shit, Tate's ready to go. Get your asses movin'," he shouted to sleepy ears. When the four of them were up and moving, Slick slammed the door and headed for the house.

In no time, particularly after Slick's wake-up, the cowhands had dressed and were in the corral saddling their horses. They walked the horses to the house, tied them to the hitching post and went inside.

Charlie Tate was waiting for them. "

Grab y'self a cup of coffee, boys, then we'll mount up," he said, gesturing to a row of metal cups and a black coffee pot hanging near the fireplace.

As they stood there with the steaming cups of coffee in their hands, Weber filled them on what they were going to do this morning. He asked if there were any questions.

"Taylor's again? I thought he didn't want to sellout? Burney said, half question – half statement.

Weber looked hard at Burney, "Charlie wants that ranch. Taylor'll sign it over, one way or another. Ya' got that?"

Colter frowned as he said, "Well, Slick, we're goin' to have trouble, that's f'sure. You know Ben Taylor's not goin' to give up his land. He's made that right clear."

"It makes no never mind, Bill," Slick said, waving some papers in his hand, "this is what it is all about. These here papers have to be signed today. Charlie's lawyer'll be here tomorrow to file them – legal-like. We'll make Taylor sign 'em and then run 'im off, or whatever it takes, ya' understand?"

"I got it," Colter whispered, and drank some more of his coffee.

Feeling he couldn't remain silent any longer, Charlie stood up and walked around the desk to face the men, "This'll be easy boys, with six of us looking down his throat, and Ben Taylor will be scared shitless. We should be back here in time for breakfast. I want them papers signed and that's it!"

Tate watched their faces as the words sunk. In the silence that prevailed, Tate thought he noticed a gleam in Joey's eyes. "Good, if there are no more questions, let's ride."

Outside, Colter checked the cinch, tightening the latigo straps. As he stepped into the saddle, he looked over at Joey Williams. Joey looked all excited. He was busy checking the cylinder of his revolver.

"You lookin' forward to this, Joey?" Colter asked him.

"Damn right I am! It'll be fun and I don't like Ben Taylor no how."

"'Jes don't do anythin' crazy, Joey," Colter warned, and wheeled his horse and the six men rode off heading north.

- - - - -

Wade was up behind the boulder and observing below. Far to the west, he could see the sun's rays just beginning to touch the prairie. Although it would be well into morning before the sun shone on his position, he thought the light had brightened considerably since his arrival. There was plenty of light now.

He was watching to the southwest, the direction Tate and his boys would come from. Damn, he figured they should be coming any minute now. Below, he could see Ben's hired man doing early morning chores. The hired hand filled two buckets of water at the pump and took them into the house.

Returning, he went to the barn where he began to pitch hay into a wagon.

Wade decided the hay was for the cattle down below. The pasture there looked over-grazed. He figured the cattle had been brought up close so they could watch them closely.

A cloud of dust began to form to the southwest. The cloud grew larger, until Wade was able to make out the riders – six of them and they were coming hard across the prairie. That's them, Wade confirmed.

The hired man, too, had noticed the growing the dust cloud. He dropped the pitchfork and ran toward the house. "Ben! Ben! Come out here quick! We got riders – comin' fast!"

In a moment, Ben Taylor was standing in front of the house. "Who do you think it is, Ben?" the hired man asked.

"I betcha' it's Charlie Tate and his boys," Ben said, peering out at the approaching cloud of dust. The riders were still too far off to identify.

"Seth," Ben asked, "Ya' still got that shotgun of yours in the barn?"

"Yep, she's still there," Seth responded quickly.

"Well, you better get it and stay out of sight – 'til we see what's goin' to happen here," Ben instructed.

Ben's wife, Anne, was now standing on the porch, watching the advancing riders. Ben turned to her and said, "Anne, you best stay in the house and keep the boy inside too. I think it might be Charlie Tate and his people. Damn, I thought we'd seen that last of that crook." Anne started to protest, but after seeing the determined look in Ben's eyes, she retreated inside.

Watching this drama from above, Wade noticed Ben was unarmed. *What the in hell is he thinking about,* Wade wondered, *to stand before six men he knew damned well will be armed. Got get a weapon,* Wade mentally prompted Ben – *go, go, you've still time!*

Instead, Ben stood there waiting. The riders were close enough now for Ben to see who they were. Damn, it is Tate and his gang of thieves, Ben thought.

Ben called to Seth in the barn, "You all set, Seth? It's Charlie and his boys and as fast as they're riding in, I'd say we're goin' to have some trouble!"

"Everything is fine here, Ben. I'm as ready as I'll ever be for trouble," Seth said convincingly.

The riders passed through Ben's gate at a full gallop, just barely ahead of their trail dust. Wade settled down behind the boulder, keeping his head down, only his eyes peering around the side. As the riders galloped into the yard, reining up hard – Wade slowly advanced the cocking lever of the Winchester . . . He was ready!

Ben stood firm, the trail dust churning and boiling up all around him. The dust was so thick he could barely breathe, much less make out the horses and riders. Finally, as the dust started to settle, Ben said,"Damn fine way to ride into a man's yard, Tate! Throwin' dust and shit all over the place!"

Tate disregarded Ben's remark about the dust. Instead he offered, "Howdy Ben, it's a good mornin' to talk some business," Tate started to step down.

"Hold it right there, Tate. I don't recall asking you to step down," Ben snapped.

"I don't give a damn whether or not you asked me to step down – I'm stepping down." Tate stepped down quickly, throwing his reins to Ed Baylor. Slick Weber stepped down moments later, letting his reins fall to the ground.

"We don't have any business to talk about, Tate. You and your cow hands best ride out of here right now," Ben told them.

That's bullshit, Taylor," Tate yelled, as he advanced to a position directly in front of Ben, "In case you don't know it, today's the day you sell me your ranch, Ben."

Chapter 11

Ben Taylor stood his ground, looking at Tate, Slick Weber and up at the cowboys. In spite of their menacing presence, Ben was neither intimidated, nor afraid. He was damned mad!

He looked each of them square in the eyes – finally he spoke, "You must have shit in your ears, Tate. I've told you a number of times that I wasn't selling my ranch! That's it! If I was to sell this place, I wouldn't sell it to the likes of you. Have you got that? Now mount up and get the hell off my place!"

Tate, his face screwed up in rage, stepped forward and grabbed Ben's shirt front, nearly lifting him off the ground. Tate pressed his face in close to Ben's, shouting as he did so, "I'm tired of your bullshit, you shit-assed excuse for a cowboy. I'm taking this ranch and you're signing the papers today and I mean now! Ya' got that?"

Ben reached up and broke Tate's hold on his shirt, pushing the heavy man out, while at the same time delivering a hard, fast right had to Tate's face. Tate staggered back for a moment then swung a right hand at Ben. Ben ducked and parried the blow with his left hand. He hit Tate again with his right, finding Tate's mouth. Blood started from the corner of the mouth, and drooled down Tate's chin. Tate put his hand to his chin and looked at the blood. He charged Ben again – more mad than smart. Ben saw him coming and side-stepped the charging figure, tripping and pushing him down as he went by. Tate skidded into the dust, face down.

Ben turned to watch Tate get up from the dust. As he did, he noticed Anne on the porch. He waved for her to go back inside. He returned his attention to Charlie Tate. Tate was up and circling around to Ben's right. He didn't see Slick Weber to his rear.

As he braced himself for another charge from Tate, he heard Anne's cry, "Ben, behind you!" He started to turn his head. Too late. The blow came hard behind his right ear, tearing his scalp. He tried to fight it, but the blackness came fast and Ben went down unconscious, with the blood from the gash flowing freely into his collar. Anne ran from the porch and knelt to care for him.

"It's about time, Slick! That asshole liked to kill me!" Tate screamed at his foreman.

Slick was standing with his revolver barrel in his hand. He'd hit Taylor squarely with the butt end. He seemed neither pleased nor upset. He looked down at Ben and Anne, "You boys were movin' pretty fast there. I didn't want ta' hit you, Charlie."

"Yeh, well alright, only next time don't wait so long."

Charlie Tate looked down at Anne, who was busy checking the wound behind Ben's ear, "Bring him around, Mrs. Taylor," Tate ordered, "he's got some signin' to do."

"That's what I'm trying to do, damn you," Anne Taylor shrieked at Tate, tears forming in her eyes.

She looked up with all the hate she could muster and said, "It won't do you any good. We're not selling. I can tell you that. Now get off our property!"

Charlie started to speak, but was interrupted, when a voice from the barn said, "Best do what the lady says boys. I gotta' shotgun here that says it might be a smart move. Now git!"

Everyone turned to see Seth standing in the doorway of the barn, shotgun leveled in their direction. The men on horseback turned their horses to face Seth.

Colter didn't like looking down the barrel of a shotgun and he made it known by saying, "Whoa there, pardner. There's no call to get excited with that there shotgun. 'Jes take it easy!"

"Shut up, Colter," Tate bellowed, "damn you boys, draw on 'im. We're wastin' time here."

Seth turned the gun barrel directly at Tate, "I'd do what the lady says, Mr. Tate. If I were you, I'd be mountin' up."

With everyone's attention centered on Seth and Tate, Joey Williams fast drew his revolver and fired at Seth. Seth staggered back momentarily and started to point his gun at Joey. Joey fired a second time, this time hitting Seth in the upper left shoulder. The impact spun Seth around and knocked him down in the door frame. He lay there motionless, half-in and half-out of the barn.

Slick Weber reached down and grabbed Anne by the shoulder. "Get 'im awake, damn it!" he yelled. Anne pulled away from him. He grabbed her again, this time tearing the front of her dress. He pulled harder on the fabric, exposing her left breast. Slick hung on to the dress and stared. Finally he said," Now lookee here, Mrs. Taylor. Isn't that a nice nipple?" and he reached down to fondle her breast.

Wade squeezed off his first round. Weber fell instantly. A bullet through the head. Next, he leveled down on Joey Williams and fired. Joey spun off the saddle and hit the ground, his revolver still in his hand. The other riders had pulled their revolvers and were looking in all directions to see where the firing was coming from. Wade fired again, knocking Ed Burney off his horse. Next he got Colter through the head and with equal precision, Ed Baylor went down and lay motionless.

In the confusion, Charlie Tate had remounted and was wheeling his horse to ride out. Wade leveled the Winchester on Tate and fired. The bullet hit Tate in the head; he slouched in the saddle and fell to the ground and the horse continued on, riderless through the front gate.

Anne Taylor was still bent over Ben. Wade could see Seth's feet were stirring. *I'd better move,* he warned himself. He slowly picked through the dust until he found each of the six empty cartridge cases. He put them in his pocket. Picking up the carbine and the branch, he moved backward in a low crouch, smoothing the dust where ever he found tracks. He moved with purpose, efficiently removing all trace of his presence.

He did the same at the overhang, where Lightfoot was waiting. When the ground was clear of tracks, he moved off, walking the horse until it was safe to mount-up and ride through the mountain saddle.

- - - - -

A curious silence loomed over the ranch yard – the quiet seeming so still, after the rapid rifle fire and men falling to the ground around her. Anne looked up from her ministrations over Ben. She turned slowly and looked up the mountainside searching for any movement, or any trace of the person who had fired so well. Nothing. No one. Where had the firing come from? She wasn't sure. She had been looking down at Ben, when the firing started. She huddled closer to Ben, more to protect him than herself. All she could clearly remember was the sound of men falling, quickly – each with a bullet in the head.

Her puzzled thoughts were interrupted as Ben began to stir. "Ben can you hear me?" she asked, whispering close to his ear. "Yes, Anne, I can hear you," he murmured, "what happened?"

"Oh Ben, I don't rightly know what happened. It all happened so fast. Tate and all his men are dead and Seth was hit. Oh Ben, will you be alright for a moment. I have to check on Seth. He's in the barn – he got hit and I don't know how bad."

She comforted Ben's head as best she could and hurried to the barn, where Seth was trying to sit up. "Are you alright, Seth," Anne said anxiously.

"I think so, Mrs. Taylor. I took some lead in the shoulder. Nothin' seems to be broken. I can move it, though it hurts like hell when I do."

"Here let me look at it and don't move it, please." She tore open his shirt and looked closely at the wound or wounds actually. There were two wounds. One was a graze that plowed a small furrow across the side of his left shoulder, while the other had entered shoulder a couple of inches from the top. She looked at his back and it appeared the bullet had gone clear through.

"C'mon Seth, do you think you can stand," she asked, offering to help him by holding his good shoulder and arm.

"I reckon I can get up. Just give me your hand for a second," he said, as he pulled himself to his feet. "There, how about that?" he asked and smiled.

"C'mon Seth, I've got to get you and Ben in the house and dress those wounds. Ben seems alright – just a little dazed.

Anne managed to get both men into the house, where she began to dress the wounds. Her young son, named Wade, helping with water and cloth for bandages. When she finished dressing Ben's head, she thought he looked like a Swami with all the bandages wrapped around his head. Next, she wrapped yards of cloth over Seth's left shoulder. When she was finished, she relaxed, put on the coffee pot and sat silent for a long time.

When the coffee was ready, they all sat around the kitchen table talking quietly as they tried to piece together the events of the morning. It was damn confusing. Ben didn't remember anything after Slick had butt-whipped him, Seth didn't remember anything after he got hit and went down and Anne didn't clearly remember what was happening, so great was her concern for Ben.

All they knew, for sure, was that an unknown person had fired from somewhere on the mountain and had neatly put a bullet through the heads of six men. It was fast and accurate. It probably took less than a minute and it was done. There were no sounds other than the rifle fire. There was no movement and nothing to indicate who it was and why they had fired. It was a strange and mysterious happening.

Ben got up from the table and looked out the window. "Seth," he said, "You think you are strong enough to help me drag those men out there into a row and maybe throw a canvas over them?"

"Now you sit down, Ben," Anne cried out, "Them fella's ain't goin' nowhere. You get your strength back first."

"Alright, Anne. Seth, we'll wait a bit, the boss and chief nurse has spoken. Someone will have to ride in for the Sheriff later on, ya' know?"

- - - - -

Wade and Lightfoot were back in the wash near the willows. Wade retrieved the leather satchel and was changing his clothes. Lightfoot had already been brushed down and cleaned well. She looked good, he thought. With the heel of his boot, he dug a hole and buried the six expended cartridges. Next he loaded six new cartridges into the Winchester. He decided he'd hide the Winchester here in the wash along with the satchel. His plan called for hiding them here until he left White Willow on his way north – then he would retrieve them. He spent a good deal of time cleaning and brushing his clothes. When he was ready, he patted Lightfoot affectionately and said, "Are you ready, "Ol Girl?" He mounted and rode toward White Willow.

As he was nearing town, he could tell from the rising sun the time was getting on to about eight o'clock. He rode slowly into town by the side street and stopped by the livery stables. He stepped down and called out," You in there, Amos?"

"Yep, I'm comin'," was the answer and Amos came out the door.

"Mornin' Amos, I left Lightfoot standing in the street all night. Plumb forgot about her! Went to Murphy's and I guess I got too many under my belt – anyways, she stood in the street all night."

"I know," he said, "I saw here standin' there and wondered where you had gotten off to."

"I think I'll take her for short ride and give her a little exercise. Maybe, when I get back, you can brush her down and give her some feed. I probably won't be ridin' out until tomorrow morning."

"Fine with me, Wade," Amos smiled and said, "Say, you better talk nice to 'er – and apologize – she's a lady, ya' know!!"

Wade laughed and rode off.

Chapter 12

It's time for breakfast, he decided, as he walked into the hotel. He found a table in the dining room and sat looking out the window. A young girl appeared shortly and took his order for ham and eggs with plenty of hot coffee. Wade felt tired, but happy the plan had fallen in place, pretty much as he had conceived it. *However; he thought to himself, I'm not out of the woods yet.*

He had ridden Lightfoot hard for about fifteen minutes and came back to town. He handed the horse over to Amos. He knew Amos would give Lightfoot only the best of care. He had inferred again, that he'd be riding out in the morning. Amos had accepted his story about leaving the horse in the street all night with ease. *The fact that Amos had noticed the horse himself, might serve his cover story well,* he thought.

Betty Chalmers stopped by his table, "I see you are up early this morning, Mr. Dellums."

"Yes, I was down at Amos Hart's, but now its time for breakfast," Wade offered, hoping to change the subject away from how early he might have been up this morning.

"Well, Mr. Dellums," she smiled down at him, "like I said yesterday morning – you came to the best place in town for good meal."

"I know that, Mam. The food here is the best I've had anywhere in my travels."

Wade could see he'd said the right thing. *Betty Chalmers glowed at his remark – she damn near blushed*, he thought.

"Well, thank you, Mr. Dellums," she bubbled, and then she turned to leave, saying, "Bye for now, enjoy your breakfast."

He smiled at her and watched her leave the room. *Nice lady*, he thought. Damn, he hoped she hadn't attached any meaning to her "up early" remark. I sure don't need anyone questioning my whereabouts today. She probably saw me coming in the front door and assumed I was up early. He decided that was the case, and put the thought aside.

His breakfast came and he ate heartily. It seemed like he hadn't eaten in days. It was probably the excitement of the morning that was giving him an appetite. He was pondering his appetite, when Sam Miller arrived at his table. "Got room for an 'ol store clerk?" he asked.

"Why sure, I happen to like old store clerks, Sam," Wade said through a mouthful of fried potatoes, "Sit yourself down. How about I buy your breakfast this mornin'?"

Miller sat down and said, "That'd be right neighborly of you, Wade."

"Heard anything from your company in San Francisco?"

"I'm on my way over to the telegraph office after I finish here. My answer should be back by now, and then I'll be over to your place with the dates and everything." Wade assured him.

"Well, what have you been up to since yesterday morning?"

"Not much really. Had my horse re-shoed yesterday and, damn, if I didn't leave her standing in the street all night. It's not the way I usually treat my horse. I was in Murphy's last night – must have had a drink or two too many, I guess.

Anyways, I went to my room and left 'Ol Lightfoot standing there.

"Well, don't fret it, Wade. I've done that a time or two myself," Miller laughed heartily, "Hell, son. That's all part of growing up!"

Wade was standing at the telegraph office counter, waiting on Chili Travers. Travers was busy at the key – a message was coming and Chili was busy deciphering the code and writing it down as the key clicked away. Finally the room went silent as the key stopped clicking. Chili touched the key a couple of times and silence again.

"Good Morning, Dellums," the telegrapher said turning in his seat. "Your answer is in – came in this mornin' Now where the heck did I put it?" Travers fished around a paper littered desk for a moment. "Ah ha!" he exclaimed, holding out the message form. "Here it is, I knew I hadn't lost it. Goin' to have to straighten up that desk one of these days."

He handed the message across the counter. Wade read it over. Great – the shipping date – tomorrow – be here in ten days – coming by rail to Idaho Falls, then on a wagon from there to here. This'll make Sam happy.

He pocketed the telegram and asked Chili if there were any charges dues. "Nope," he smiled, "Your boss on the other end paid for it. Have a good day, Dellums."

"Thank you, Chili," he replied and left the office.

- - - -

Ben and Anne were pulling the canvas over the six bodies. It had been quite a chore, dragging each of the bodies over to the corral side and placing them side by side in a grisly row. Seth had brought a canvas from the barn. With the gruesome job completed, Anne looked at Ben, "Ben, I'll ride to town for Sheriff Todd."

"Honey, as much as I hate for you to have to make the ride, I'm afraid you're elected. Seth can't ride with his shoulder the way it is and I'm too dizzy yet to make the ride."

"That's alright – I don't mind. For god's sake, someone's got to fetch the Sheriff - and we have got to get these horrible bodies out of the yard. I'll get into my riding clothes," and she hurried into the house.

Ben turned to his hired man," Seth, how's the shoulder? Any better?"

"Oh, it 'jes hurts like hell, Ben," Seth reported, holding his shoulder gingerly, the red of blood showing through the makeshift bandages.

"Let's get Anne's horse and see if we can get 'er saddled up."

They were struggling with the cinch when Anne came back dressed in her ridding clothes, boots and hat. She pushed the men aside and finished the saddling of her horse. She led the horse to the house porch where the two men were now sitting.

"I'm ready now, Ben. I'm bringing the doctor back too. I want him to look at both of you," she said with determination.

"I don't know that we need the doctor," Ben started to argue, but noting the resolve in Anne's eyes, he decided to let it go, "Well alright, probably a good idea — be on the safe side right Seth?"

Anne smiled, stepped lightly up into her saddle and headed the horse out, increasing speed so that by the time she cleared the gate, the horse was at a full gallop.

The two men watched her until she was nothing but a dust trail in the southern prairie.

- - - - -

Wade was resting on his bed, both arms up behind his head. The rest was needed before he went across to Sam Miller's place with the telegram. Getting up, he changed into his spare shirt. As he was buttoning the shirt front, a woman's excited voice could be heard down in the street. She was calling for the Sheriff. He went to the window and peered through the thin curtains. It was Ben's wife - and, yes, she was very excited.

"Sheriff Todd," she called again and jumped down from her horse and started for the door to the Sheriff's office. As she did so, the door opened and a large, older man stepped out.

"What is it, Mrs. Taylor?" he asked as she ran into his arms. Holding her by both arms, he asked again, "Slow down, Anne. What is it? What's wrong?"

She stopped, put her hand to her throat for a moment, collected her thoughts and her breath, then she began, as calmly as she could, to tell Sheriff Zachary Todd about the events as they happened at the ranch this morning. When she told the Sheriff about the mysterious rifleman, he scratched at the back of his head, tilting his hat some, so that it lay practically over his eyes. Readjusting his hat, he asked about the condition of Ben and Seth. She said they were alright but she wanted the doctor to come out and look at them.

"Anne, I'll get my deputy and we'll ride out to your place." He turned to a man standing next to him, "Ed, go find Marty, will ya'?" and the man rushed off to find Marty Stillwell, the deputy.

"Sheriff, you'd better bring a wagon, we've got six dead men out there," Anne said, her voice calmer now, her eyes steady. "Oh, and Zack, could you send for the doctor too. I'm worried about Ben and Seth. They need a doctor's attention bad."

"Don't worry none, Anne. We'll get the doctor." He sent another man scurrying off to find Doc Martin. Todd put his arm around Anne's shoulder and led her toward his office. "We'll wait inside, Anne, until we get everyone rounded up."

Wade watched the scene below with interest. He had stayed back from the window so no one could see him watching. He sat on the bed later and wondered about what he'd seen. Sheriff Todd seemed fairly calm about the shootings, perhaps it was because he had to calm Ben's wife in order to get some factual information from her. He recalled Sam Miller saying Sheriff Todd was a good and fair man, not given over to unnecessary gun play. He had brought order to White Willow with little use of his gun.

In a few minutes, he could hear voices in the street again. He looked down to see the Sheriff and Ben's wife mounted and ready to ride. A wagon was coming and the man on the seat with a badge on his shirt front must be the deputy, Wade figured.

A buggy pulled up a moment later. From the dress of the man, Wade decided, that must be the doctor. When the wagon and buggy caught up, the group turned and rode south out of town, the Sheriff and Mrs. Taylor in the lead.

A gaggle of onlookers were still standing there watching the Sheriff's party ride out. They started to scurry off in a number of directions. Wade knew they would be all over town telling their gossip about the big shooting at the Taylor place.

Looking in the mirror, Wade adjusted his hat and, telegram in hand; he nonchalantly walked downstairs and across the street to Sam Miller's store.

On entering the store, he could see Sam talking with a small group of folks at the end of the long counter. Wade stopped and stood aside as all salesmen do when their customer is talking with his customers. He could tell from the animated conversations – two men kept gesturing excitedly – the conversation had to be about the shootings. Finally, Sam noticed Wade and broke away from the conversations and walked over to where Wade was standing.

Wade held up the telegram as if to say, "it's here, Sam!' He started to talk, but Sam interrupted him.

"Did you hear about the shootings, Wade?"

"No Sam, what shootings?"

"There was a shooting this morning out at Ben Taylor's place. Charlie Tate and all his boys are dead. They were shot by an unknown gunman, or so they think, because no one saw who did the shooting."

"Damn, Sam, that's a terrible thing. What was it all about?"

Miller hooked his thumb over his shoulder, "Ed there," indicating with his thumb again, "says he thinks Tate was tryin' to run Taylor off his land. No one seems to have any details. Sheriff's riding out there with Mrs. Taylor right now. She rode in to get 'im."

He stood there silent, offering no questions or answers – after all, he's not supposed to know these folks. Finally, Wade said, "That's a terrible thing, Sam."

Sam looked thoughtful for a moment, the agreed, "Yes, yes, it is! Damned shame the way some people act, isn't it?"

He shook his head a little, as if to clear his mind and looked at the telegram.

"I see you got your answer here," as he read the telegram. As Sam read the telegram, Wade thought, *well, business must go on – shooting or no shooting. A little death here and there never seems to slow the wheels of commerce, does it?*

Miller studied the telegram, then he smiled, "This is fine, Wade. A confirmed order and delivery in ten days. Ya' can't beat that with a stick, can ya'?"

"Like I said before, Sam – the firm I work for is reliable. They've been in business a long time and know the value of honesty and good service. It makes my job a lot easier, I can tell you."

"More companies ought to think like that. I surely appreciate you taking the time to send for the confirmation and all. I know you didn't have to do that."

"Well, I wanted to, Sam. A man should know when his goods are comin'."

"Wal' thanks again. I suppose you'll be ridin' on now?"

"Yep, I kinda' hate leavin' White Willow. It's a right friendly town."

"You're right about that – even with this shooting, it's still a neighborly place. Looking at the bright side, ya' might say the shooting today 'jes rid the barrel of some rotten apples.

They shook hands and, as Wade was about to leave, – Sam scratched his head and wondered out loud, "Damn, now whatta' my goin' to do with those saddles Tate ordered?"

Chapter 13

Seth and Ben were still resting in their chairs on the front porch. Ben's son, Wade, was playing in the yard, as if it had been just another day around the ranch.

Seth was the first to notice the swirl of trail dust to rise up from the prairie floor. "They're comin', Ben." he said, pointing with his good arm.

"Looks like she got the Doc too," Ben murmured as he squinted to see the riders.

They stood waiting to greet the Sheriff's party as it thundered through the gate. Ben had his arm over his son's shoulder.

At the gate, Anne and the Sheriff slowed their horse, forcing the wagon and buggy to slow. The dust slowly settled. They rode on in to the house.

Ben and Seth walked out to greet them. Seth taking the reins from Anne and the Sheriff and Ben shaking the hand of the Sheriff as he stepped down.

"Sorry to hear you had this trouble, Ben," the Sheriff said with a look of concern, adding, and "I'm glad to see you're alright."

"Thanks, Zack, I'm 'jes a little shaken and dizzy, that's all." Ben explained, pointing to his bandaged head.

"Can you tell me what happened?"

"As much as I can remember – it all happened so fast." Ben went on to explain that Tate and his boys had showed up early – that Tate was raving on-and-on about wanting the ranch. Tate wanted Ben to sign the papers, right then and there. Tate grabbed him by the shirt front and a fight started. Several punches were thrown. The last he remembered was Anne's shouted warning, and then everything went black. When he regained consciousness, the six men were down and dead, Seth had been shot and Anne was holding him and sobbing.

The Sheriff turned to Seth, "What can you tell me about this, Seth?"

"Wal, Sheriff, I was watchin' from the barn. Tate's people couldn't see me. Up to that point, it all happened the way Ben said. Anne yelled at Tate, saying that the ranch wasn't for sale and they'd better got off the place. She was on the ground holdin' Ben. Slick gave 'im a pretty good hit with the butt of his revolver. I stepped out from the barn with the shotgun leveled and told them they had better do what the lady asked. Colter was uneasy about having the shotgun pointed at him. He tried to talk me out of firing at him. Tate was yellin' to his boys, telling them to draw on me. I pointed the gun at Tate – that's when Joey Williams fast drew on me, grazing my shoulder. When I tried to put the gun on Joey, he fired again hittin' me solid in the shoulder and I was down real fast. By the time I had my senses back and was able to move, the shooting was over. Tate and his people were all down. I guess I should have never pointed the shotgun at Tate and kept a better eye on his boys." Seth finished.

The Sheriff was scratching his head, "Anne, throughout the shooting, you were on the ground with your back to the mountainside, caring for Ben, right? Did you at any time look back to see who was firing, or where it was coming from?"

"No, Sheriff, when the shooting started, that's when Weber ripped my dress and was going for me. I saw Weber go down right next to us. I huddled down over Ben trying to protect him. God, he was helpless! I wasn't sure what was happening, but I didn't want Ben or me to get hit. Tate's boys were falling one after another. Zack, it happened so fast! The last to fall was Tate, after he had mounted his horse and was trying to ride off. The shooting stopped and it was so quiet. I didn't move for quite a while, for fear that whoever was shooting might shoot me if he saw some movement. When I finally did move, I looked up at the mountainside, but I saw no one, nor did I see any movement up there. It's a mystery, it is!"

"Sure seems that way, Anne," Todd said, turning to his deputy, "C'mon Marty, let's see if we can find any tracks up there. Have any of you gone up there since the shootings?"

Anne said, "No,' she hadn't, and both of the men shook their heads to indicate they hadn't either. The Sheriff and his deputy marched up the hill.

"Marty, you check off to the left there and I'll check to the right. We're looking for tracks, empty cartridge cases and anything else that doesn't belong there. Check everything real careful," the Sheriff instructed.

Down low they found carved sticks and several wooden toys, play things for the young boy, the Sheriff figured. They moved higher to where the large boulders were. The boulders would provide good cover for gunman. They searched and searched, but found no trace of a person's presence. The ground showed no markings or tracks. "Check the rocks and boulders, Marty, for scratches or any kinda' marks," Todd yelled to the deputy, "if someone was up here, they had to leave some kinda' track. Look carefully, Marty."

They tracked back and forth, up and down the mountainside for the better part of an hour. They had switched sides in the hope that if one man missed something, another man might discover it. They found no tracks a man might make. The only tracks they did see were animal tracks – deer mostly, and a large cat track that looked to be a bobcat or a mountain lion. Probably tracking the deer, the Sheriff reasoned. Finding nothing, they walked back down.

Sheriff Todd knocked on the door and entered, Marty following behind. The doctor was working on Seth's shoulder, cleaning the wound with an antiseptic.

Ben stood, his head now encased in a well-fitted bandage, "What'd you find, Zack?"

"Not a darned thing. It sure puzzles me how a man could go up there and not leave a track or a clue to his presence. All we spotted were some animal tracks."

Marty looked at Anne, "you'd almost think it was a ghost up there, doin' the shootin', Mrs. Taylor."

"How's that possible, Zack? Anne is dead certain the firing came from the mountainside. Not only that, but the way Slick Weber fell indicated the shot came from that direction."

"I know what you're sayin' Ben - but there's nothin' up there – not a trace, Todd said, shaking his head.

"This is a mystery then!"

"Well, the Sheriff started slow and thoughtful, " I think what we have here is a very smart shooter. Someone who had it in for Tate – probably followed Tate and his boys out here and put them down. Picked up his empty cartridge cases and wiped out his tracks. Left quietly and hopefully is on his way to parts unknown by now. Let's face it, Tate wasn't liked by most folks around here, not that most people go around here shootin' people in the head, mind ya'. Nevertheless, it's all possible, isn't it?"

Ben Taylor had to agree with the Sheriff 's reasoning. But why?" he asked, "why our place?

"If I were to take a guess, I'd say the situation presented it self well. A fight goin' on between you and Tate. His boys sittin' there watchin' the fight, not really covering themselves. It could be a perfect situation to drop them all – unawares. The speed of the firing shows there was no hesitation. No love lost for any of them."

Anne entered the conversation, asking, "What now, Zack? Is there anything we should do? We certainly didn't do the shooting. God knows, we might have had a good reason to, considering the fact that Tate was trying to run us off our land."

"Well, don't you worry any, Anne. I'll continue to look into the shootings. Who knows, we might get a clue and find the shooter. Although, with no clues, I doubt if anything'll ever come of it – at least, that's the way I see it now. Keep that under your hats. I don't want folks knowing my true thinking just yet."

Doc Martin was just finishing the sling he'd made for Seth's left arm. "There you go – how's that feel, Seth?" he asked as he fiddled, adjusting the fit around the elbow.

"Feels great Doc, ya' think I'll live?"

"I'd say to a ripe old age. There's no doubt about it, as long as you don't go pointing shotguns at folks, that is!" Doc Martin laughed, putting his arm over Seth's right shoulder.

"Doc, I'd like you to come outside and check the bodies with me, if ya' will?" Sheriff Todd gestured to Marty, "C'mon Marty – we are goin' to load 'em in the wagon."

The three men approached the long canvas cover, the deputy kneeling and pulling the canvas away. They stood and looked at Charlie Tate and his cowhands for a moment. The doctor leaned over and checked Tate's pulse. He found none, then he turned Tate's head, viewing the bullet hole the entered from the rear left and exited from the right front of his forehead. There was a large exit hole in the forehead. "Probably dead before he hit the ground, I"d say, Zack

He moved over and looked at Colter's body. Dead with a shot straight in the nose, a large exit hole at the back of the head. As they moved down the line of bodies, the results were essentially the same – dead, shot through the head.

The Doc straightened and commented, "Looks like this feller – the shooter, was an excellent rifleman. The wounds are from a rifle, I'd imagine."

"That's right Doc, I figure it'd have to be a rifle if the shots came from where I think they came from," and the Sheriff smiled and continued, "Shit, that narrows it down doesn't it? Every one in the County has a rifle or two!"

"You do have a mystery on your hands, Zack," the doctor said, touching Todd on the arm, "I guess I'll be gettin' on back to town. You have Marty bring the bodies over to my place, by the back way, and I'll make the arrangements."

"Thanks, Doc, I appreciate your comin' along."

Todd and the deputy began lifting the bodies into the back of the wagon. The Sheriff was afraid, at first glance, there might not be enough room without putting one body over another. He felt it might not look well, having the bodies all stacked like that. However, they were able to squeeze the bodies into two rows of three. They fastened the wagon tailgate and walked to the house, just as Doc Martin was getting into his buggy, having said his goodbyes to the Taylor's.

"See ya' in town, Doc," Marty said as the buggy started out.

Anne and Ben were on the porch," Get 'em loaded alright, Zack?"

"Yep, we're all loaded. No problems. You don't mind if we borrow your canvas, do you? Marty forgot to bring ours."

"Naw, go right ahead. I can pick it up sometime when I'm in town."

"Fine, it'll be in my office," the Sheriff assured. He sent Marty back to place the canvas over the bodies.

The Sheriff looked over to the corral, noticing four horses standing with their saddles on, "Those Tate's animals?"

"Yes, I put them in there to get them from under foot. They were milling around the yard. Tate's horse and another ran off, out the gate," Anne said in explanation to Todd's question.

"Well, hang on to them, Anne, 'til I figure out what's to be done with them. Don't know whether or not Tate had any family. We'll keep an eye open for the other two. If we see 'em, I'll try to run them down."

Todd mounted his horse and leaned down to shake Ben's hand. "You take it easy now. See ya' the next time you come to town. Sorry about all this."

"Thanks Zack, I don't guess there much need to feel sorry. I s'pose we all should feel sorry for Tate and all his greed. I can't say I'll miss the man, all things considered."

"You're right, Ben," with that said, the Sheriff wheeled his horse and started out for the gate, Marty and the wagon trailing behind.

Anne and Ben stood there watching them go for a long while. With arms around each other, they finally went into the house.

Chapter 14

The large clock on the wall read one-forty-five when Wade went into the dining room. He asked the young waitress if he was too late to eat. She assured him he wasn't and handed him a menu.

"Great." He said, taking the menu, "what do you suggest?"

"Our Blue Plate Special's good. Today, it's chicken. You know, just the kind that mother used to make. I think you'd like it. You get all the trimmn's too."

"You sold me; I'll have the Blue Plate Special."

Ned Chalmers came into the dining room, spotted Wade and came over to his table. "Did you hear about the shooting?"

"Yes, I heard a little about it over at Sam Miller's place. No one seemed to know much about it. I guess they were waitin' for the Sheriff to come back."

"That's true. I guess the Sheriff's due back any time now. I've heard all kinds of things this morning. - from a band of bandits doin' the shootin', to some drunken Indians shootin' up the Taylor ranch. Ya' can't hardly believe the things ya' hear. I don't think Ben Taylor would kill anyone. It's probably smart to wait 'til the Sheriff gets back and let's us know what really happened."

"I think you are right there, Ned. This mornin' I saw a number of people runnin' around tellin' folks what was goin' on. From what I gathered at Sam's; nobody knows what really happened, other than Tate and his boys are supposed to be dead."

"I agree. What are you havin', Wade?"

"I just ordered the Blue Plate Special."

"Good, you'll love it. It was my mother-in-law's favorite recipe. See ya' later, gotta' get back to the bar."

-- - - -

Sheriff Zack Todd rode slowly into the south end of town. Marty was behind him in the wagon. He could see a group of people gathering in front of his office. *Damn curiosity seekers,* he thought, *I'll bet the town gossip's runnin' high right now.* He smiled at the thought of the many tales that are probably circulating around town.

He reined-in at his office, the crowd milling close to him. "Now stand back, folks." He stepped down and turned to face the excited townspeople. A tall man stepped forward and asked, "Can you tell us what happened out at the Taylor's, Sheriff?"

"Not a lot to tell, folks. Tate and his cowhands were at the Taylor ranch, tryin' to force Ben and Anne off their property. Tate was tryin' to make Ben sign over his place. They knocked him unconscious and shot their hired man – you all know Seth Johnson – in the shoulder putting him down. Tate's foreman, Slick Weber tore Anne's dress and it appeared he was goin' to have his way with her. Anne said she he might've raped her at this point. At the mention of the word rape, the townspeople looked shocked. Several of the women present put their hands to their mouths in disbelief.

The Sheriff continued, "All of a sudden, Weber was hit and fell dead, a bullet through the head. No one saw the shooter. Marty and I spent more'n an hour on the mountainside looking for tracks and we couldn't find any trace at all. It seems we have a bit of a mystery with this one."

A woman asked, "How are the Taylor's? Are they alright?"

"Yes, Mrs. Burton, they are. Anne was unhurt, just her pride shaken; Ben took the butt-end of Weber's revolver to his right ear. Doc says he has a slight concussion, but will be fine. Seth took a bullet to his left shoulder. It went clean through. It hurts but it will heal. Actually, they were lucky – Tate and his boys weren't. They're all dead, a bullet to the head."

Todd answered a few more questions, then asked the folks to move along, "Please folks, break this up. Marty has to take the bodies over to Doc Martin's now." He motioned for Marty to move the wagon out, and he walked into his office. Slowly the gathering in front of his office broke up, talking between themselves as they went.

- - - - -

Wade stepped out of the hotel's front door. Looking to his right, he could see a group of people in front of the Sheriff's office. The Sheriff must have come back, he thought, as he noticed the gathering breaking up, folks walking off in a number of directions. He turned left and walked down to Murphy's Saloon.

"A good afternoon to you, Wade," Murphy offered cheerfully, "How are you this fateful day?"

"I'm fine, Mike. What do you mean "fateful?""

Mike looked surprised, "You mean you haven't heard about the big shootout at Ben Taylor's?"

"I did hear some mention about it at Sam Miller's earlier, but no one seemed to know much about it."

"That's true, but the Sheriff has just come back. We should be hearing what happened real soon."

Two of the men who had been a part of the group in front of the Sheriff's office came into the saloon. A crowd of bar customers gathered around them as they told what the Sheriff had reported moments ago. Murphy walked down and listened for a bit, asked a few questions, and came back to Wade.

"He poured a shot, as he told what the Sheriff had said. When he finished, he puzzled for a moment and said, Can you beat that? A mystery gunman. That's hard to believe, isn't it?"

"It is hard to believe. You say the Sheriff said he couldn't find any tracks of the gunman?" It is hard to believe that man could move in and get away, without leaving some kind'a tracks."

"Well, that's what the Sheriff said. Claimed he and the deputy looked all over the mountainside for more'n an hour and found nothin' - ya' know, Wade?, Tate had a lot of enemies. Most folks didn't like him. Who knows who could have done it?"

Murphy walked off again, serving drinks along the bar. The bar had filled since the Sheriff's return. Wade stood there, shot glass at his fingertips, deep in his thoughts – perhaps all the planning is beginning to pay off, his mind reasoned. *I'm glad I thought to pick up the cartridge cases and brush out my tracks.*

His mind thought about the killings for the first time. *He knew he wasn't a killer and yet, he'd just killed six men with ease. Well, not with ease, he reminded himself, but he had fired just the same.* Rationalizing a bit, *he told himself the men were bad and what they were trying to do was equally as bad. Maybe he should have given them a chance. No, not against six armed, angry men. No, he had handled it right – fast and accurate – all over in a minute.*

His mind continued, *they'd of made Ben sign away the ranch, then killed him, raped his wife and made sure the hired man was dead too. They would have all been dead, including the boy, if Wade hadn't been there. That's the only way to look at it,* Wade decided, *besides Ben's my pardner and you don't let anything happen to a pardner. If you can damn well help it.*

Mike Murphy made his way back again, bottle at the ready. "They say Slick Weber was about to rape Anne Taylor when the shooting started. Weber was the first to get it – right through the head. Damn, what a shootout! They say the gunman only fired six shots, every one of them through the head. Damn, whoever he was, he damn sure didn't waste any bullets, did he?"

"Nope, Mike, it sure sounds like he knew what he was doin', that's f'sure." Wade nodded in agreement.

Mike looked up and said, "Hi Sam," as Sam Miller leaned into the bar, next to Wade. There were a few empty spaces left at the bar now. The talk along the bar was of the shooting.

Sam said, "Howdy Mike, Wade," he nodded to Wade. He looked down the bar, and said, "I can tell from your bar the Sheriff's returned. Better pour me one, Mike."

Miller turned to Wade and asked," Well, Dellums, how do you like our White Willow now?"

"I still feel the same way, Sam – it's a nice town, only now it has a mysterious gunman that shoots the bad guys. Not a bad idea, really, every town ought to have one. Might keep folks law abiding," Wade offered, suppressing a giggle.

Miller and Murphy snickered at the remark – finally, Sam Miller agreed. "You know, you just have a point there. Every town ought to have a gunman – a sort of one man vigilante, who doesn't have to worry about the law. A kind of Robin Hood who shoots out the bad guys and disappears into thin air. Probably wouldn't need a Sheriff any more," He laughed heartily and downed his glass of whiskey in one gulp.

Wade confessed, "I was only kiddin', Sam."

"Oh, I know you were young fella' It does tend to get rid of the bad guys, doesn't it? Probably have to take this up with the town council – see what they think?" he laughed again, patting Wade on the shoulder, "Well, boys, I gotta' get back to the store. You leavin' today, Wade?"

"No, I decided to leave in the mornin' See you next trip."

"Hey, Murphy," Wade asked after Sam had left, "What happened to the Taylor's?"

"Oh, they're alright. Ben got butt-whipped in the ear pretty bad and Seth, that's their hired man, he took a bullet in the shoulder. Sheriff says it went clean through, so's he'll be alright when it heals. And Anne wasn't hurt none."

"That's great; I heard they're nice folks. Hell, I guess it was Sam that told me that."

"Well, Sam was right. They're just hard working folks, scratching to make their ranch pay its way. Funny thing, though – ya' know Ben's nickname is "Two Dog's" – no one

97

seems to know what it means or where he got it. He won't tell, only that he got the name as a boy."

"Two Dogs, huh, that's a funny nickname," Wade laughed; more to himself than to Mike's remark.

Mike ambled off, pouring shots and cajoling his customers into having another drink. You could hear his hearty laughter above the din of the bar.

When he returned, he was laughing. "The boys down the bar told me there's a good side and a bad side to this shooting. They say the bad side is that I just lost some good steady customers and the good side is – I don't have to put up with Tate's drunken cowhands no more. No more fights and shootings. Maybe they're right, but it has been my experience that someone'll show up to take their place. Liquor seems to do that, ya' know."

"Probably true, Mike. You don't have too many sober men, pickin' fights these days, do you?"

"I guess that's true," Murphy said with resignation. He quickly poured Wade another shot, put up a second glass for himself and filled it. He raised his glass and toasted, "Well, here's to their replacements, where ever they may be!" He touched his glass against Wade's and downed the shot.

Wade laughed.

Chapter 15

The next morning was a very sunny and warm Thursday. Wade made preparations to leave White Willow and head secretly for "Two Dog's" ranch.

There were a number of things he had to do before he could ride out of town. First, he'd have to get Lightfoot and Marybelle from Amos Hart's and settle up with him. Then, he'd have to check out of the hotel and pay for his room. He'd have to pack the pannier for the mule. He reminded himself he had only one pannier, the other being hidden in the wash north of town. He'd get the hidden one when he headed north, on the way home to the Bitterroots.

No sense going crazy trying to get everything done at once, perhaps I'll have breakfast, get myself organized and let the Chalmers see I'm in no rush to leave White Willow. He washed, dressed and went down to breakfast.

"Good Mornin', Mr. Dellums," Betty Chalmers chirped, as he came down the hotel staircase.

"Good Mornin ', Mam," Wade said, touching the brim of his hat.

"I trust you slept well, Mr. Dellums."

"I sure did, Betty." He wished she'd call him Wade, instead if Mr. Dellums. "I had a couple of drinks with Ned last night and went up to bed. I feel great this mornin'. Now I need a good breakfast."

Betty smiled as Wade walked into the dining room. *Nice man,* she thought.

It seemed like no time and Wade was back at the hotel desk. "Betty, I'll be leaving today – probably check out a little later. I'm hoping you can have my bill ready. There's no big rush, I haven't had my breakfast yet and then I have to get my horse and mule from Amos Hart. So, it'll be a while – I just wanted you to know."

"Oh, sorry to see you leave so soon, Mr. Dellums. Don't worry none; your bill will be ready when you are."

"Thanks, Betty," and he returned to the dining room.

Wade walked down to Amos Hart's livery stable after breakfast. He found Amos cleaning out some of the stalls.

"Good Mornin', Amos."

Hart looked up at Wade, leaning his pitchfork against the stable wall, "Good Mornin' to you Dellums and it's a fine morning, isn't it?"

"I'm leaving this morning, Amos. I need Lightfoot and Marybelle – and your charges, of course.

"Well, let's get your critters out and see what we got here." He turned and went into the stables.

Wade went in and grabbed his saddle and tack, taking it outside. Amos came out with Lightfoot. Wade saddled the horse. Next, came Marybelle. Amos began putting the pack saddle on her.

"S'pose ya' heard about the shootin' out at Ben Taylor's place?"

"I sure did, Amos, wasn't that somethin'?"

"Sure was. Marty, the deputy was in here yesterday. Said it was like the shooter was a ghost, can ya' believe that? Said there were no tracks, no nothin'. Well, the Sheriff had got hisself a mystery. To tell the truth – I don't think Sheriff Todd's goin' look too hard for the shooter. He's probably glad to see the likes of Charlie Tate gone, that's what I think. Can't say I blame him much, they don't pay him to be a Pinkerton."

Wade laughed easily, "You might be right there, Amos."

When the animals were ready, Wade paid Amos and led the horse and mule up the street to the Hotel.

Back in his room, Wade laid out the canvas and placed half of the sample rifles at one end. He carefully turned in the edges and rolled the rifle in the canvas, making a tight package. He secured the mantie with rope, tying each end and the center tightly.

Starting on the second mantie, he realized he was short one rifle, the one he'd cached away north of town. He decided he'd put his personal rifle – the one he usually carried in the scabbard along side his saddle – in the mantie. It was necessary to keep the load on the mule even, the same weight on each side. So far so good!

He packed the remaining pannier. Stuffing as much of his things as he could in it, he found there some items left over, things that wouldn't go into the leather satchel. No problem, he'd put them in his saddlebags. He wondered if anyone would notice that he had only one pannier. He doubted anyone had paid much attention to him when he was unpacking the mule last Monday. If that were the case, then they'd pay even less attention to him now as he packed his mule for the trail.

Wade took the two manties downstairs first packed and secured them well on Marybelle... Next he brought down the pannier and the saddlebags, plus those items he planned on tying to the back of the saddle. He finished packing the mule, checking to see that everything was tight. He placed the remaining items on Lightfoot, and went into the hotel lobby.

"I'm all set to go, Betty," he said as he approached the desk. "I guess it's time to square up and be off."

"Like I said, your bill is ready," she said efficiently, pushing the written bill across the desk. "You were here three nights at a dollar a night – that's three dollars."

"Thanks Betty, I sure enjoyed staying here." He pushed three silver dollars across the desk. "You can bet I'll be back the next time around." He picked up the bill, folded it and shoved it into his vest pocket.

"You're always welcome here, Mr. – Wade interrupted her with a slight wave of his hand, "Please call me Wade, Betty. Mr. Dellums sounds so formal."

"Alright," she said, "You're always welcome here, Wade, and she smiled at herself as if she were getting away with something she shouldn't.

"Thank you Betty," he said and left the hotel.

Stepping up into his saddle, Wade turned Lightfoot to the left, holding Marybelle's lead rope with his right hand. They walked slowly to the corner, where they turned right and headed down the street. As they passed the barber shop, Wil Grant waved. Wade waved back and headed south out of White Willow.

Wade was a little nervous as they walked out of town. *Damn,* he thought, *why am I nervous now? My plan worked. I'm not a suspect – so why am I worrying?* He wondered about the feeling, but couldn't put any meaning to it. About a mile out of town, he relaxed in the saddle. He looked back, no one was following him. "Damn," he shouted to no one, "so far so good." He spurred Lightfoot a little, urging her to pick up the pace.

Two miles out of town, when he felt no one from town could see him – he turned the animals west, heading for the mountains. They took their time, finding another wash similar to the one they used north of town. They walked most of the way to the mountain in it. When they were in the foothills, he turned Lightfoot north onto a trail that led to the pass.

The southern pass was at a low elevation and quite wide. Wade marveled at how easy this pass was, compared to the higher and narrower one to the north. "So far so good," he whispered, when he ridden through the pass and encountered no one making its passage.

The sun was high in the sky as he rode south along the valley floor. He spurred Lightfoot again. He wanted to appear as a man in a hurry – a friend fervently responding to a friend's call for help. It wasn't long until Ben's ranch visualized in the distance. It crossed his mind that he was riding the same trail that Tate and his boys had ridden early yesterday morning.

It'll be good to see 'Ol Two Dogs. It has been too long. Damn, how long has it been? At least six or seven years, I'd guess. Ben wasn't married and now he's married with a young son. Where does the time go?

With the pressure of the shooting over and gone from his conscience and the town of White Willow behind him, Wade began to feel the excitement of seeing Ben building inside of him. That feeling had come to him a number of times as he sat behind the boulder above the ranch house but there was nothing he could do about it then. Now – soon, he could and the idea suited him well. He spurred Lightfoot on.

Wade slowed Lightfoot when he rode through "Two Dog's" gate, he could see Marybelle was in agreement with the slower pace. She never liked to gallop, but she'd walk forever if you asked her to.

There was no one outside as he neared the house. – Then Ben stepped out of the barn. Wade could see him looking over, a bit wary of a stranger riding in. He continued watching Wade ride in, his body alert and skepticism in his eyes. Wade slowly lifted his head so that the wide brim of his hat no longer covered his face.

Ben's face changed from apprehensiveness to total surprise. "Wade!" he screamed and charged over to meet him.

"Damn Wade, you did come! Good to see ya', Pardner!" he was yelling as Wade stepped down. Ben grabbed him and hugged him hard.

"Well, "Two Dogs", here I am! How the hell ya' been?" Wade, grabbing Ben and hugging him. He looked at Ben's bandaged head, "Damn fella', you been fightin' in a war or somethin'?"

"Naw, I had some trouble yesterday – I'll tell you about it in a little while,"he confessed, then he called out, "Anne, c'mon out here! Wade's here, Anne!

Anne came out and ran over to the men. She threw her arms around Wade, "Oh, it's so good to meet you Wade. Ben has told me so much about you.

Wade stood taller and with false dignity, said, "Well now, you must be the new schoolmarm, Mam," then he laughed full and hearty for the first time in a long time.

Ben was laughing too, as he introduced Wade, "Anne, I'd like you to meet my 'ol pardner, Wade Dellums. Wade, this is my lovely wife, Anne."

Anne was smiling excitedly as she said to Wade, "Ben said you were quite a joker. I can also tell you the local schoolmarm is very attractive, so you paid me a right nice compliment."

Swinging his hat wide, Wade took a deep bow, Áh'm at youh suhvice, Mam!" He laughed again.

Ben looked at Anne, "Where's 'Lil Wade?" They both turned to see the boy standing sheepishly on the porch, obviously shy in front of a stranger.

Anne called to him, "Wade, come over here and meet your Uncle Wade. C'mon now, don't be shy."

"C'mon son, come meet your Uncle Wade," Ben coaxed.

The boy started over slowly, coming to his mother's side, one arm around her leg. Wade offered his hand to the boy. Ben coaxed again, "C'mon son, shake hands with Uncle Wade."

The boy leaned forward; extending his small right hand, his left still firmly wrapped Anne's leg, and shook Wade's hand uncertainly. "Well, how are you, Wade?" Wade said, shaking the boy's hand some more. "I like your name, Wade is it? Sounds just like mine. I like that! "Then he kneeled down to the boy's level and hugged him. The boy relaxed in Wade's arms and broke into a big smile, "Howdy, Uncle Wade, Daddy's told us a lot about you."

"He did, did he? I sure hope he didn't tell you any fibs about me."

Anne beamed as she explained, "Wade, we named him after you. "Lil Wade'll be five later this month. He's big for his age. Goodness, he's growin' like a tumbleweed and he's underfoot like a tumbleweed too." Wade could see the proud mother in Anne as she went on about the boy.

"C'mon, Big Wade and 'Lil Wade, "she said, grabbing their hands. "You arrived just in time for dinner. It is just about on the table. Ben call Seth - its dinnertime and she marched the two Wades into the house.

Chapter 16

They had finished eating and were sitting at the table over steaming cups of coffee. Seth had gone to care for Wade's animals.

Ben was asking about when Wade had received his letter in Montana. Wade explained how he had read the letter, gotten a little sleep, loaded up the mule and horse and ridden off to Ben's. He had added a few days to the story to cover the time he'd spent in White Willow.

"How come you brought Marybelle?" Ben said, looking a bit puzzled.

"Well, Ben, I guess that's the salesman in me. Thought I'd come prepared, in case someone wanted to buy a Winchester or two. Always anxious to turn a dollar, ya' know."

It was Wade's turn, "C'mon Ben, tell me about the trouble you had yesterday? Damn, you and Seth look like you just fought the Indian Wars. I'm dyin' to know what happened."

"Well Wade, you're never goin' ta' believe this," Ben started and went into a detailed account of the events of yesterday morning... Anne picked the story after the part where Ben went down unconscious. She described how Seth was shot and gave details of the shootings – how the men were falling to the ground, left and right. Finally, she recounted her ride to town to gather up the Sheriff and Doc Martin.

Ben went on to explain how the Sheriff and his deputy had combed the mountainside looking for any sort of clue to the unknown shooter, but had found nothing. When they had finished telling their story, they both looked a little worn and drawn. "I tell 'ya, Wade," Ben concluded, "it's a damned mystery to us and the Sheriff is just as puzzled as we are."

"Was this Charlie Tate the trouble you wrote about?"

"He sure was! Damned man kept pesterin' to get this ranch. We told three or four times that we were goin' to sell to him or anyone. It never seemed to faze him. He just wanted this ranch, no matter what. I'd say yesterday he came for a showdown and planned to take the ranch by force."

"This whole story is hard to believe. How did he think he could take your ranch by force?"

"He had this lawyer fella' from Idaho Falls, who'd come and file the title papers properly. It always looked legal. Tate had done this a number of times. He'd run-off a few of our neighbors, adding their ranches to his. He wanted to become the biggest rancher in these parts, I guess."

"Tell me, Ben, would you have signed those papers?"

"No, I believe I wouldn't have. Except if they had gone to hurt Anne or the boy, I jes might have. I guess we'll never know the answer to that one, will we?"

'Sounds to me like Tate and his people were a bunch of bad ones. You're lucky to be alive, if my guess is right. Looks like your unknown shooter saved your bacon, doesn't it?"

"He sure did. I wish I knew who he was; I'd really like to thank 'im. We were in a bad way about the time he started firing, I can tell you that."

"You should be thankful you weren't killed, 'Ol Pardner," Wade said, putting his arm around his friend.

"Hell, Wade, let's go up the hill out back and look it over – ya' never know, we might find a track or somethin'"

"Alright, let's take a look.

Ben went to Anne, who was clearing the dishes from the table. He told her where they were going. The two men left and walked up the hill.

They searched around for a while, finding nothing but Sheriff Todd's and Marty Stillman's footprints in the dust. Ben pointed to several large boulders, "I figure the shooter was behind one of these. Hell, he could see everything that was goin' on down there, from right about here."

Wade nodded, knowing for sure that Ben was right.

'How do you think the shooter escaped, Ben", Wade asked, looking up the mountainside.

Ben looked north and south, wondered a bit, then said firmly,"I think the shooter escaped along that trail there, "he said, pointing south. "I'll betcha' he got away in that direction."

"Hmmmph!, "Wade grunted, 'you're right about this bein' a mystery. It kinda' boggles the mind, doesn't it?"

The two men looked at one another for a moment, then as if in silent agreement, they turned and walked down the hillside.

Reaching the foot of the hill, they noticed "Lil Wade standing near the corner of the house. He'd been watching as they searched the hillside.

"Did you find anything, Uncle Wade?" the boy asked.

"No "Lil Wade. We didn't find anything, just the Sheriff's tracks."

"Oh," the boy said, sounding a little disappointed. Then, he brightened and smiled, saying, "Do you want to see my pony, Uncle Wade?"

Wade bent down and looked into the boy's eyes, "I sure do. How about you show me your pony?" Wade straightened and looked at Ben.

"Go ahead, Wade spend some time with the boy. Be good for him to get to know his uncle. I'll help Anne with the dishes."

"Alright, "Lil Wade," Wade said, taking the boy's hand, "let's go see that pony."

They walked across the yard to the corral, hand in hand, the boy half-skipping to keep up with Wade's long strides. It occurred to Wade that he'd never spent much time with small children. Having no brothers and sisters, there was no nieces or nephews to spend time with. It's a new experience, he thought, and feeling the small hand in his own, he agreed in his mind that it was a pleasant one at that.

The boy broke loose from Wade's hand, slipping through the corral rails and ran to the back of the corral. A well-shaped brown and white pony was standing there. By the time Wade had climbed into the corral, 'Lil Wade had led his pony over.

"Say there, that's a darn fine pony you have there, 'Lil Wade."

"He sure is, Uncle Wade," the boy beamed as he threw his arms around the pony's neck, hugging it. Isn't he purty, Uncle Wade?"

"What do you call him?"

Mommy calls him "Purty Boy" – so I guess that's his name, 'cause he is purty. We got him a couple of weeks ago. I just love him!" the boy smiled and hugged the pony all the harder.

Wade sat down in the corral with his back to the inside of the rails. The boy joined him. The pony looked down on them both. The two Wades, man and boy, sat there for a long time, talking about the boy's life on the ranch. What did he do everyday? He played and sometimes he helped Seth with the chores. Now he has a pony to care for and that will keep him plenty busy or, at least, that's what his Daddy had told him.

Wade liked and enjoyed the boy. He was amazed at how bright he was – only five years old and he could talk the leg off a grown man. In the back of his mind Wade felt it was time for him to have a family and maybe a son like 'Lil Wade here, who knows? He gave out a little chuckle, thinking here he was wanting a son, and he didn't even have a wife.

"Lil Wade stopped talking when he heard the chuckle from Wade, "What are you laughing about, Uncle Wade?"

"Oh nothing, 'Lil Wade, I was thinkin' how nice it would be to have a son like you, that's all."

The boy smiled, Thank you, Uncle Wade."

"How're you cowpokes doin', down there?" a voice said from above. Wade looked up to see Seth standing behind him, his good arm over the rail, a broad smile on his face.

Wade stood and with a little bluster, said,"Wal, me and
'Lil Wade here have been having a man-to-man talk. Ain't
that right, 'Lil Wade?"

"You betcha', Uncle Wade," the boy smiled once again,
perfectly at ease with Wade now.

"The shoulder givin' you much trouble, Seth?"

"Naw, the bullet went clean on through. The wound
hurts a little once in a while, but its nothin' a man can't
handle. I s'pose Ben and Anne told you all about the shootin'
yesterday mornin'?"

"Yep, they 'jes told me a while ago, you folks were darn
lucky to get out alive."

"That's right. If it weren't for that mysterious shooter,
we'd a been goners, that's f'sure."

"Have you been with Ben long?" Wade asked, wanting to
steer the conversation clear of the shooting.

"Let's see now, a couple of years, I guess."

"Ben's lucky to have you helpin' him," Wade suggested.

"Hell No! It's the other way around. I'm lucky to be
workin' for him. They're darned fine folks. Well liked
hereabouts too." Seth returned with enthusiasm.

"Seems right – I know folks always liked Ben back home
in Montana."

Seth was silent for a moment, then he said, "Ya' know,
Wade. I used to live up your way there in Montana. Some
years ago, I lived around the Stevensville town. Had a small
farm and did some ranchin' too."

"Heck, Seth, you were right in our neck of the woods.
My place is about fifteen miles north of Stevensville. Ben's
parents live nearby. How long since you left?"

"I'd guess it was fifteen years or more since we lived there.
I had a small ranch here too, my wife and I, but I sold it
before I came to work for Ben. It was after my wife died."

"I'm sorry to hear about your wife's passin', Seth."

"She was a good woman, I miss her a lot. We never had
any children, so after she passed on, I couldn't see any reason
to keep a ranch. I sold out and came to work for Ben and
Anne. I kind'a enjoy being around the boy."

"I understand the feeling, Seth," Wade confessed, the boy
is a little charmer, isn't he?"

"Yep, he is that. He's my little helper sometimes with the chores. We work and he talks and we do have ourselves a time out here."

"It's funny, when you came up behind us, I had been thinkin' about how nice it would be to have a son like him, then I had to laugh, 'cause I'm not even married."

Seth chuckled, and with a wink, said,"Well then, Wade, I guess you know what you gotta' do first, don't ya'?"

Chapter 17

The sun was low in the western sky. The supper dishes were done – everyone had pitched-in so Anne could be free on the kitchen chores. The five of them were sitting on the front porch; talking and watching the sun do its afternoon color show.

Anne asked, with curiosity, about Wade's life – about how it was traveling around the West, seeing all the towns and places she'd never seen, She wondered too, she said, "Isn't it a lonely life?"

Wade had never been one to talk of his life. He was surprised at the ease he felt when he began talking about how footloose he had felt at the beginning. It was fun to go to places he'd never been to, just seeing different people and places – even the hotels he stayed in had been fun, at first.

He described his first trip to San Francisco. How amazing it was with all the buildings and the many people in the streets, and of the countless dives and saloons. He told them the story of how he had gone to the waterfront one night.

Three men had grabbed him, pulled into an alley and tried to rob him. Luckily, he fought his way free and ran like the wind, he said, "Otherwise, I would have been found dead in the alley, come mornin'."

He told them of the many small towns and of the people. He found most folks decent and friendly. He said he'd seen two shootings that took place in saloons, both over card games. He spoke of the numerous fights he'd also seen, again in saloons.

"One time in Utah, some boys robbed the bank. The whole town lit out after them, catching them with the loot, about five miles out of town. Turned out one of the boys was the banker's son, who was afraid to ask his father for some money, so he and some of his friends decided to take a "quick" loan from his father's bank."

Anne interrupted, asking, "Wade, you said this was all fun at first, what about now?" Wade could feel the womanly concern in her question.

"The truth is, Anne, it's not so much fun anymore. You get so every town looks the same as the one before it. Hotel rooms are probably the worse times, 'cause you're all alone in them and they all tend to look and feel the same. You meet the same kind of man in this saloon that you met in the last saloon. Usually, they are troublemakers of one sort or another. With every customer you call on, you tend to give the same sales talk you gave your last customer. You mouth the phrases that have worked before. The Winchester tends to pretty much sell itself, which makes my work easier; however, it's repetition, the same words over and over."

"The worst times for me, is when I am in the saddle between towns. You can talk to your critters only for so long. The rest time you sit your saddle and think and think about you life."

"The trouble with thinking about your life so much, is you think; for example, that maybe its time for me to marry, settle down, have some kids and a nice place. You sit there some more, thinking as always, and you start to think about the other side of the idea. Maybe I should travel even more – go East and see what's goin' on there. Travel some new trails, ya' know? So you think and think, pretty soon you are more confused than when you started. You think, I don't want to think about it anymore and you don't until the next time you are in the saddle between towns." Wade was surprised to hear himself saying the things he'd thought about so much in his travels.

"Hey, I'm doing all the talkin' here," he said looking at the others; who were watching him, their eyes intent and listening to every word he had said. Feeling a little embarrassed to be the center of all this attention. Wade said, "Let's change the subject, please?

"Well, Ben, Anne said, with a grin,"Sounds like you got to find Wade a schoolmarm, doesn't it?"

"Yep, that's what we gotta' do – find my 'ol pardner a nice little schoolmarm and get him all hitched up. What do you think, Seth?"

"Hell, Ben, I already told him that down at the corral this afternoon."

Then, they had a good long laugh!

"Let's go inside," Anne suggested, rubbing her hands on her upper arms, "Its getting cold out here."

Once inside, Anne lit several lamps as everyone sat down at the table. Wade rummaged around in a drawer at his desk and produced a bottle of whiskey. He poured the men a drink. He settled down in a chair and started talking about when he and Wade were boys growing up together.

"Wade, ya' remember 'ol man Harmon down at the store and the time he caught us swipin' his dill pickles? We had to sweep out his store for a week as punishment. He told our parents, so there was no way we could back out, and he had the dustiest store in Missoula County, ya' remember that time, don't cha' Wade?"

Wade chuckled, "I sure do and all the time we were sweepin' the floor, we were snitchin' more pickles and crackers. Our little punishment cost 'ol man Harmon a good deal more than the original two pickles we swiped."

With a surprised look on her face, Anne said, "You boys shouldn't be talking like that in front of the boy. That's not the sort of thing to be teaching him."

"Aw, Anne, all boys do a little of that – it's all part of growin' up. It won't hurt the boy none to hear about it."

Ben wasn't to be stopped. "Wade, how about the time we played hookey from school and got caught? Ya' remember that? We snuck away from school and went to our favorite swimming hole on the South Fork of the Clark River. Darned if Sheriff Tilson didn't catch up with us and caught us swimmin', bare butts an all."

"Ben!" Anne cried, looking down at the boy.

"Alright Anne," he said, then to Wade," You do remember that time"

"You betcha', I remember the day. He took us back to school and we had to sit there in our wet clothes, 'cause we didn't have anything to dry ourselves with. Our parents found out about it too, didn't they?"

Anne leaned forward, saying, "Since you two boys want to remember the good old days. Maybe you can tell me, Wade, where did Ben get that silly nickname "Two Dogs?"

Wade could feel Ben staring daggers at him. He paused, taking his time to answer. *I'll remember my promise, Ben,* he thought, *but I do have to answer the question.* Finally, Wade said, "I don't rightly know where he got that silly nickname, but I do know something that I'll bet you he never told you – it's about his proper name."

"Knowing Ben, you know he hasn't told me much about his name, certainly not about "Two Dogs", that's f'sure."

"Has he ever told you about what the "T" stands for in - Benjamin T. Taylor?

"No, in fact, he has never told me there was an initial in his name. Has he got a middle name?"

"He sure does! He could see Ben's eyes were shouting, "Shut up, Wade!"; however, Ben knew that this was a tradeoff for not telling the meaning of "Two Dogs" Wade dragged out the silence for a moment and said, "The middle initial stands for Throckmorton." At the mention of the name everyone howled. Seth was slapping his leg with his good hand and arm.

Ben began to laugh too, guarded at first, then easier, more relaxed. "Ya' know," he admitted, "That silly name has haunted me since I was a tadpole. I asked my Dad one time, why they had named me Throckmorton, and he told me Mom's great-grandfather was called Throckmorton. She had only met him once or twice before passed. She had liked him and that's how I came to be called, Benjamin Throckmorton Taylor."

Ben refilled the men's glasses and they settled down to talk of the difficulties he and Anne had encountered in building the ranch to what it is today. Severe drought one year, sub-zero blizzards the next. When it wasn't the weather, it was grasshoppers wiping out the hay crop, or a skeptical banker who could be counted on to lend them far less than was actually needed to carry the ranch through the season.

According to Anne, they never lost faith in the ranch and their efforts to make it succeed. They had scrimped and saved, working all the harder. She said, "It was even a more bitter pill to swallow when Charlie Tate came nosin' around wantin' to buy the ranch. Where was he in the years we were really struggling?" she cried, "Had he come during those early years, we might have sold-out. Although, I doubt it, ", she smiled.

Anne put young Wade to bed in their room and his bed was made up for Wade. The adults continued to talk into the night, renewing their friendship and sharing experiences with one another. It was well after midnight when the lamps were snuffed out and everyone went to bed.

Wade awoke to the smell of fresh coffee and the strange sensation of a small finger poking at his shoulder. He opened his eyes to see 'Lil Wade standing next to him, poking away with his little finger.

'Good mornin', 'Lil Wade. How are you today?"

"It's time to get up, Uncle Wade. Mommy says she's got hot coffee ready and, guess what? She's making flapjacks and sausages!"

Wade dressed and was sitting on the edge of the bed, pulling on his boots, when the boy returned. He was carrying a cup of coffee. "Well now, pardner, Thank you," Wade said, "Sounds to me like you like flapjacks and sausages?"

"I sure do, Uncle Wade," and he ran out to the kitchen area where the flapjacks and sausages were being cooked. Wade followed him out, joining the men, who were already at the table, their fingers wrapped around steaming cups.

After breakfast and when the men had left to do the morning chores, Wade offered to help Anne with the dishes. It was the first time they had been alone. She talked of what life with Ben was like here on the ranch, and how 'Lil Wade was growing so fast. Wade smiled and said nothing when

Anne said; "she had met Ben at a Grange Social in Salmon."
"Ben always liked to go to these Grange Socials when he was back in the Bitterroots," Wade told her, with a broad smile.

"Anne, I'm afraid I'll have to be leave in a little while,"Wade told her, as she was finishing the last of the dishes.

"Leaving? Wade, how can you be leaving so soon? You just got here!" She said, surprise in her voice.

"Truth is, Anne, I've got to get back to my ranch. Winter is comin' and I have to help my foreman get the ranch ready. I know I don't have to tell you about winter in these parts."

"God knows you don't have to remind me about winter, Wade. Ben'll be so disappointed. You sure you can't stay, even for a short while."

"I haven't spent more'n six or seven days around the ranch since last May. I really do have to get back. Besides, the trouble Ben wrote about is gone; you really don't need me to help anymore. I'd best be getting' back."

"I'm going to miss you, Wade. I can see you have been a good friend to Ben all these years. 'Lil Wade will miss you too. You can see he's taken quite a shine to you, can't you?"

"He's a fine boy, Anne. I don't think I've thanked you for naming him Wade. It's an honor to be his namesake."

Ben came in the house and Wade broke the news of his departure. "Damn Wade, you just got here!" he stammered, the news unexpected.

"Ben I'll be back in the Spring, then we'll have all sorts of time to spend together. Right now, my ranch calls and as you know, ranches don't wait."

"I s'pose you're right. I'm damned glad you came, no matter what," he said, and he hugged Wade tight.

Chapter 18

"We're headin' home, Marybelle." he said to the mule as he swung the pack saddle onto her back, adjusting the sawbuck tree to just the right place on the blanket pad. He reached under and secured both of the cinches. 'Lil Wade came up and said, "Are you really leaving, Uncle Wade?"

"I'm afraid I have to go, son," Wade admitted.

The boy's face clouded with disappointment, "Are you coming back soon?"

"Yes, I'll be back to see you in the Spring. Then we can have fun together. Maybe we'll go riding together, how about that? Say, have you got a saddle for your pony yet?"

"No, Daddy said when I get a little bigger, he'd get me one, and then I can ride "Purty Boy."

"Well, I tell you what - I just happen to have a fine pony saddle back at my ranch. When I come back in the Spring, I'll bring it and you can have it, what do you say to that?"

He could see the excitement in the boy's eyes, "Gee, Uncle Wade, would you do that? I could ride my pony then, Golly, I'd like that. Oh, thank you, Uncle Wade."

Wade adjusted the mule's breast collar then went to work fastening and adjusting the breeching. The boy watched as Wade packed the manties on the pack saddle. Wade took great care to see they were tied securely with rope.

When he had finished with the animals, Wade reached into his vest and brought out a silver dollar. He flipped it in the air and caught it quickly. He handed it to 'Lil Wade. "Here, Wade, a silver dollar from me to you. You save it and sometime when you are in town with your Dad, buy something nice for "Purty Boy".

The boy's eyes shone, as he turned the shiny coin over and over in his small hand. "Golly, I never had a silver dollar before. Am I rich now, Uncle Wade?"

Wade laughed and reassured the boy, "Yes, you are, pardner — you are very rich for a young boy."

Lightfoot and Marybelle were standing in the yard, saddled and ready for the trail. Wade was saying his goodbyes to his good friends.

Ben and Wade walked to the horse, Anne was standing back. When Wade was in the saddle, Ben stepped forward, offering his hand. Wade leaned down and grasped his friend's hand. He pulled Ben closer and whispered, "Don't say anything, Ben — just listen. No one in White Willow knows we are friends. Remember that. You understand?"

He dropped Ben's hand and sat up in the saddle, ready to spur Lightfoot on to movement. Ben said, "I'm not sure, Wade. What does that mean?"

Wade looked down at his pardner and said, "Think about it, Ben!' and rode off.

After about fifty strides, Wade stopped and turned back in the saddle to look at Ben and Anne. He called out and waved, saying, "So long for now. It was good spending two days with you, Two Dogs!" He turned forward in his saddle and spurred Lightfoot on to a canter, Marybelle reluctantly picking up the faster pace.

Anne and Ben stood there, waving and watching their friend ride out the gate.

"What did he mean, Ben? He didn't spend two days with us."

Ben was still waving his hand, his eyes trained on the figure of his boyhood friend riding off.

Ben turned to Anne and held her tight. With a look that showed he now understood Wade's last remark, Ben smiled and told Anne, "I think I just figured out what he meant and it's something that we'll have to talk about later!"

He looked into her eyes and saw a tear start down her right cheek. Together, they turned and watched Wade ride into the distance — soon, all they could see was a growing cloud of trail dust.